The Missing Agent

A 1920s historical mystery

A Dora and Rex Mystery
Book 2

Lynn Morrison

Marketing Chair Press

Cover design by DLR Cover Designs

Published by

The Marketing Chair Press, Oxford, England

LynnMorrisonWriter.com

Print ISBN: 978-1-7392632-2-5

Contents

To my daughters - I will always be so proud of you both.

Chapter 1
The attempted break-in

L ord Rex hunched behind a shrub in the garden of a stately London home, and for once, a woman wasn't the cause of his strange behaviour.

Well, not entirely, anyway.

Under the cover of night, the nearly bare fronds of the weeping willow tree swayed in the gentle breeze, casting dancing shadows across the lawn. Thick hedges lined the pebble-strewn pathways, standing like sentries at watch over the home's inhabitants.

It wasn't fear of being caught that made Rex hesitate. With his blond hair hidden under a hooded cloak, even someone who knew where to look would struggle to pinpoint his location.

No, the concern weighing on his mind wasn't so much *breaking in* as breaking a rule. As a member of England's upper crust, he'd had society dictates drilled into his mind since the day he was born. One of the earliest guidelines he'd learned was that gentlemen always use the front door.

But, if Rex hoped to best his mentor by beating her inside, he had to rely on his war training. As a messenger, he'd learned that the most direct route was usually the most dangerous.

Getting from place A to B safely required him to examine all possible pathways and choose the one least travelled.

At this late hour, his best option was to enter through the kitchen. From there, he'd run the below stairs gauntlet, evading detection by the few servants still awake, and slink up the back staircase to the bedroom that marked his destination. It had seemed a smart enough plan on paper, but staring at the lit windows on the main floor, he questioned whether he had overlooked a better alternative.

A light tread pricked at Rex's ears, alerting him to new arrivals. The time for doubts and second-guessing had reached an end.

A pair of strapping young men, dark-haired identical twins just shy of the age of twenty, stepped into the shadows to flank him on either side. Besides years of experience navigating London's mean streets, their few extra inches of height gave the young men further advantage. Standing between them, Rex felt like a squat tome shelved between matching bookends.

Archie, physically distinguished only by a wayward freckle beside the corner of his mouth, tilted his head in Rex's direction. "The cook's the only person left in the kitchen. The rest of the staff have either turned in for the night, or, in the case of the butler and head housekeeper, disappeared into their office with a fresh pot of tea. If you still plan to go through with this, now's your best chance."

Rex nodded his agreement, but his limbs refused to comply. He was in the middle of giving himself a silent, but very stern talking to, when the other twin whispered a question.

"Want me to do another check, guv?"

"No, Basil, that isn't necessary. We'll go now. Keep close and step lightly," Rex added. He lifted his right foot and swung it forward before he could second-guess himself again.

Rex avoided the path, knowing just how loudly the loose

stones crunched underfoot. His blue eyes were sharp as a cat. He crept along the grass, using the hedges to hide his progress, until all that remained were the last steps to the kitchen door.

He grabbed Archie's arm to get his attention and then motioned for him to split off to the right. Archie did as instructed and aimed his feet toward a small shed. He didn't look back until he had collected a metal pail and a trowel from inside it.

Rex raised his hand high enough for Archie to see and lifted three fingers. He matched his breath to the countdown in his head. Three. Two. When he hit one, he lowered the last finger, signalling for Archie to proceed with the plan.

Archie swung his arm forward, back, and forward again until he launched the pail onto the stone path. It hit with a clatter and rolled raucously until it finally bumped up against the hedge.

Seconds later, the cook swung the back door open wide and marched out with a rolling pin in her hand. She waved it menacingly and shouted, "Oi, foxes! Be gone with you!"

Archie, still out of view, sent the trowel flying even deeper into the garden. That was all the encouragement the cook needed. Mumbling curses under her breath, she marched up the pathway to deal with wayward beasts that plagued London's private gardens. With her back turned, she did not notice Rex and Basil sneaking through the now open kitchen door.

The two men glided through the kitchen area, taking care not to bump into any of the shelves of food stores or the stacks of pots and pans. Unlike the upper floors, the cook's domain lacked electricity. A single gas lamp burned low, and the rest were out. Burners and tall ovens lined one wall. Under the rear window was a large basin with clean dishes stacked beside it. A wooden table dominated the middle of the room.

Rex noticed little of this. He motioned for Basil to stay

behind him, and then he peeked around the edge of the doorway. The hallway was clear, just as expected. However, the door to the butler's office stood cracked open, allowing a narrow beam of light and sound into the corridor. If Rex wanted to reach the stairway to the second floor, he'd have to pass in front of it.

There was no choice. He had to go for it.

"Stay close," he mouthed to Basil. He tiptoed into the corridor and promptly stepped into a spot of water. His right leg slipped sideways, knocking him off balance. Basil grabbed him around the waist in a most undignified manner, but in doing so, saved him from bumping against the wall.

Rex's heart thumped so loudly he could hear its echo in his ears. If this were the war, he'd be long dead.

He shoved that thought aside and focused on catching his breath. Basil tapped him on the arm to point out the new problem. At the other end of the hall, there stood a mop and a bucket. The faint sheen of puddles dotted the floor, not yet fully dry after the final cleaning.

Rex glanced down and nearly gasped when he saw the streak of mud he'd left across the floor when he'd slipped. He was supposed to remove his shoes before walking across the hard stone floor. He bent over to untie his laces and heard the hinges of the kitchen door squeak.

Basil shoved him forward, sending Rex onto all fours.

Rex's hands and knees stung from where they'd hit the hard floor. He'd be bruised tomorrow, but if he got caught here, a few bumps would be the least of his worries. He scurried forward, crawling on his hands and knees, feeling the damp seep through the legs of his trousers. When they passed in front of the partially open door, he held his breath.

Somehow, they made it to the other end of the corridor without being discovered. Still, the seconds flew past. The cook could emerge from the kitchen at any point. There was no time to dawdle.

Up the stairs the men went, as fast as they dared while still keeping light on their feet. Rex opted to walk only on the front part of his foot, even though doing so made him feel utterly ridiculous.

His mentor would never end up in this situation. He was sure of it. She'd have remembered to untie her shoes outside, and to slip them off as soon as she came into the house. With her grace, she'd likely have danced down the corridor instead of crawling like a young babe.

Recriminations circled in his mind as he climbed the second flight of stairs until he reached a closed door. There was no knob to turn. He had only to tug on the brass handle to pull it open.

Rex turned around to check that his partner in crime was ready for the next stage of their infiltration. They'd passed unseen through the servants' domain. Now, on the upper floor, the risk was being seen by a member of the resident family. Dressed, stained and bruised as he was, that might even be worse than being caught by the head housekeeper, a known termagant who ruled with an iron fist.

Basil motioned for Rex to get on with it.

Rex gave a gentle tug on the handle and the door swung toward him without issuing the slightest sound. Unlike the kitchen door, the servants kept these hinges oiled.

A thick red carpet lined the polished wooden floor, running from one end of the hallway to the other. At least here he didn't have to worry about someone hearing their footsteps. The deep pile of the carpet absorbed all sound, providing for a quiet environment. After all, it wouldn't do for a heavy-footed servant to wake their master before it was time to rise.

Rex's destination was the fourth door on the left. He knew the board outside the door squeaked if you trod on the right edge of it. Other than that, however, there was little to prevent him from arriving without anyone taking notice. Neither the floral arrangement on the hallway table nor the tall grandfather clock ticking the hours would raise any alarm.

More importantly, there was also no sign of his mentor. Despite it all, he'd clearly got the jump on her. Twenty feet and his journey was at an end. Rex couldn't wait to settle into the wing chair by the bedroom fireplace and warm his hands while his mentor caught up.

Rex moved the door to make a bigger gap and took the last steps into the hallway. The need for haste won out over that for caution. Rex darted across the final stretch.

The doorknob was within reach when something grabbed onto his leg. Pain shot up from his calf as claws sank into his flesh. He yelped, stupidly, and barely bit back a litany of curses, all aimed at the marmalade cat wrapped around his leg.

The cat's eyes glittered in the electric light. It hissed at Rex and then reared its head back and bit him on the knee.

Any last dredges of caution flew away with the wind. Rex abandoned his stealth and grabbed hold of the knob, twisting and shoving with no regard for safety. He stumbled into the bedroom with the cat still attached to its prey.

A very unladylike snort of laughter was the only reward Rex got for his inhuman show of restraint.

There, in the very wingback where he'd planned to relax, sat Theodora Laurent. It was more accurate to say she was draped across the chair, with her legs dangling over one armrest. The glass of ruby Port in her hand was testament to how long she'd been waiting.

"Mews! Get off me," Rex growled at the furry beast who'd attacked him. He leaned over to pry the cat loose, and the animal had the gall to swipe at his hand. He jerked his hand back, this time uttering a curse, and watched tiny beads of blood rise along the mark.

That proved to be Dora's undoing. She and Basil both burst into laughter, uncaring about any risks of being overheard. Although it wasn't exactly appropriate for Dora to be in Rex's bedchamber, she trusted Rex's grandmother to turn a blind eye.

When Rex finally coaxed the cat into letting him go, he deposited the little beast onto his bed and turned around to face his mentor.

"How did you get here ahead of us? I stood in the garden for half an hour. I'd have seen you if you went past."

Dora wagged a finger at him. "Silly man. Why go to all the trouble to sneak past the servants when the front entrance was unguarded?"

Rex spluttered. "The front entrance? You came in through the front door? But it was locked! Barred, even, at this hour!"

Dora rolled her eyes at his indignation. She straightened up and motioned for Basil to help himself to the wine. "Rex, dear, when did you first learn about this challenge?"

"Yesterday," he answered, his eyebrows wrinkling in confusion.

"That's right. And in the interim, you had a full day of access to the house. You could have prepared any number of entry points. Personally, I chose to flip the latch of the far right window in the drawing room. You know the one I mean. It has a lovely bush growing in front of it. All I had to do was wait for a lull in the passing cars, slide the window up, and slip inside. From there, it was a straight path up the main staircase to here."

Dora smiled to lessen the blow of her words, but it was no use. Rex growled at himself for his stupidity. He abandoned all propriety and dropped onto the bed, newly enraging Mews in the process.

"Give me one reason I should keep going, Dora. You've

7

been training me for months now, and I can't even break into my home without getting caught."

"I hardly think the cat counts," Basil said helpfully, earning an eye roll from Rex.

"You know what I mean." Rex balled his hands into fists and rested them on his knees. "I was a soldier... a messenger, no less. I must have driven along every road in Northern France. Yet, my experience doesn't make a darn bit of difference now. Say it, Dora. I'm a world class screw-up and I'm going to get someone killed."

"You are not," Dora countered. She got up, set her glass aside, and crossed to perch beside her student. "Your only flaw is that you keep forgetting we are not at war. You aren't a soldier on a mission, but more of a cat burglar needing a fast path both in and out."

"But Basil and Archie agreed with my plan..."

"Basil and Archie are not you," Dora said, interrupting Rex. "They are trained servants. It's as obvious as the nose on your face that their first thought would be to go through the kitchen. They do what they can, but sometimes we need people who can use the front door. That's where you and I come in."

"Where you come in, maybe," Rex grumbled.

"Where we both come in. Trust me, Rex. There will be places where even I can't go inside and roam freely. It's why I suggested that Lord Audley recruit you to our team."

"She's right, guv," Basil added from his seat in front of the fire. "Besides that, you're overlooking the obvious. Even though you didn't exploit your advantages, you still made it here. And if we're being honest, Archie and I would never have had the courage to break into a hotsy-totsy place like this if we weren't with you."

Rex lifted onto his elbows and shifted his gaze between

Dora and Basil. He searched their faces for any signs they were putting him on. All he found were smiles of encouragement.

Dora's grin widened. She patted him on the shoulder. "Tell you what, old boy. I'll give you a second chance to best me tomorrow night."

Rex cocked up his eyebrow. "Sneaking into here again?"

Dora batted aside that idea. "What would be the fun of that? I've got something much better in mind." She wiggled her eyebrows at him. "Let's see which one of us can make it into Clark's bedroom first."

Rex dropped back down and groaned again. "That's hardly fair, Dora. Between your looks and Clark's infatuation, we both know that if you want into Clark's most private of domains, all you have to do is ask."

"And that, my dear sir, is me using all my advantages," Dora replied. She punctuated her statement with a gaudy wink.

Chapter 2
This calls for drastic measures

Dora pulled the wool coat tighter around her body and watched the drizzle run down the front windshield. Even though she had dressed in a warm coat and high-waisted trousers, she hesitated before getting out of the car. Not even knowing she'd be late for her appointment could induce her to go before she was ready.

Her best friends in the world sat in the front seat. Harris had one hand resting on the steering wheel, while he draped the other arm around Inga's shoulders. His fingers drummed a tune that only he heard.

Inga twisted in her seat until she looked Dora in the face. "Can you get a move on it already? If you don't get out soon, the bar will call last orders before Harris and I set foot inside. Unless you want Harris and me to accompany you into Lord Audley's, you'd better get a move on."

"The flask I saw you tuck into your handbag should be enough to tide you over," Dora countered. "Your threat has little teeth as I'd just as soon you came along with me. He's going to ask me how Rex is getting on, and I'm not sure what to tell him."

"Have you considered being truthful?"

Dora crossed her arms and glowered at her friend. "In my line of work? Don't be ridiculous! Besides, it isn't Rex's stalled progress that has me worried so much as me not knowing what to do about it. We built a robust training programme, and he's completed every step of it. And yet..."

"None of us want to see him dead." Inga's voice softened. "That is your concern. Am I not correct? Freddie got in over his head and paid for it. You're worried... scratch that. We're all worried that Rex might get hurt."

Harris turned in his seat so he could join into the discussion. "We can come up with more training exercises. Why not ask the old man if we can let Rex break into his home? Or, even better, one of his investment properties? I'm sure Audley owns plenty of London real estate."

Dora considered the suggestion, but soon discarded it. Not that it wasn't valid, but how much testing should a person do? Whatever the limit was, Dora felt sure they were getting close. Rex needed something different. The what, however, escaped her.

Still, Inga was right. Lingering overlong in the car would not bring Dora any closer to a solution. She did her best thinking on her feet. If her luck held, having Lord Audley put her on the spot might be just the push she needed to come up with an answer.

Dora leaned forward and bussed Inga on her cheek, leaving a trace of lipstick behind.

"Hold up! That's my job," Harris scolded, although his words didn't carry any heat.

Dora shimmied in her seat and kissed his cheek as well. "There. Now you're even. Enjoy your night out and don't worry about me getting back home. I'll make my own way."

"You always do," Inga chimed. "Like a stray dog we can't chase away."

Dora paused with her hand on the door handle and turned back to her friend. "If I'm the stray, what does that make you? The ever-loyal hound? If so, can we tie a ribbon in your hair and pretend you're one of those poodles?"

Inga swatted at her, and Dora rushed out of the car, laughing under her breath. If nothing else, she'd managed to beat back the doldrums that had been threatening all day.

Feeling lighter despite the dreary October weather, Dora flipped up the collar of her coat and hurried around to the side entrance to Lord Audley's London abode. The door to the coal stores was unlocked, just as she'd expected. In short order, she made her way through the house and into the private sitting room that overlooked the rear garden.

Audley was waiting inside, sitting in the middle of a sofa, surrounded by a sea of loose sheets of paper and folded newspapers. He'd slicked his grey hair back from his face. Once held in place by pomade, it now showed signs of him running his hands through it. He'd used the same substance to twist the ends of his moustache. His glasses magnified his bloodshot blue eyes and did little to hide the bruises underneath. Both were testament to his exhaustion.

Dora balked in the doorway, choosing to rap on the frame instead of her normal march in. "Is this a bad time?"

Audley gave a tiny jerk of his shoulders at the sound of her voice. He coughed to hide that she'd startled him and told her to come in. "This whole month is fast becoming a bad time, so there's no point in you coming back later. Take a seat."

Dora shrugged off her coat and draped it over the back of a wooden chair. Before sitting down, she topped up Audley's glass of scotch and poured one for herself. "Is it the Turks again?"

Audley pulled his glasses off and massaged the bridge of his nose. "I half wish that it was. At least with them, I know where to look. Instead, I've hit nothing but stone walls of silence. But that isn't why I've called you here. I want to see how you and your protégé are getting on."

"We're getting along well?"

Audley dropped his hand from his face and glanced up. "Why did you end that with a question mark? Before tonight, you'd had nothing but positive remarks to make."

Dora gritted her teeth in frustration with herself, mostly. Honesty wasn't her forte. Nothing for it now except to carry on with the conversation.

"Lord Rex has completed the agreed training programme, to my satisfaction. His final test was to break into his own home and make it upstairs into his room without being caught." She bit her lip and fudged the last bit. "He passed with flying colours."

"I'm not hearing a problem with that. What am I missing? Or, should I say, what are you leaving out?"

Dora took a sip of her drink while she gathered her thoughts. Although she enjoyed every opportunity to get the best of Lord Audley, he hadn't risen to the post of the king's spymaster for no reason. Instead of searching for a way to outwit him, perhaps now was the time to take advantage of his wit and experience. She twisted the glass in her hands, watching the reflection of the firelight in the liquid.

"He has mastered all the needed skills. He can pick a lock, scale a wall, and even identify the worst of Inga's poisons."

Audley waved her on.

"The problem he has is one I cannot overcome," she blurted. "Rex still thinks like a soldier. He is too used to following orders, and relies on his old methods rather than face challenges head-on. Worse yet, even though we've all reassured him, he can't stop comparing his skills to my own. It's no contest, but try getting him to believe that."

Audley set his glasses on the side table and retrieved his

drink. "What do you propose? Shall I locate another trainer for him?"

Dora shook her head. "I can't see that helping any more than what we've done. It will simply be one more person who is better at spying than he is." Dora's words trailed off as an idea flashed in her mind. "He needs to be in an environment where he has no choice but to operate in plain sight and rely on his wits. More importantly, it must be something with low enough stakes that we won't overly stress him from day one, yet where his unique skills can shine. Of course, finding that perfect case is likely more improbable than Rex getting his confidence up on his own," she mumbled.

"I wouldn't be so sure about that," Audley said, interrupting her. "I may have a way we can both achieve our ends with a single solution."

Dora leaned forward, enrapt. "I'm listening."

"I need a new man in Parliament to assist with my current dilemma."

The word new snagged Dora's attention. "What's wrong with your existing man in situ?"

"Nothing, per se. However, he's been at this for several weeks now and has made little headway. The lack of progress grates on us both. His actions are getting more and more daring. Just the other night, he was nearly caught searching an office in the House of Lords."

Dora shuddered. "That is a gutsy move, and I can see why you'd be concerned. Westminster is certainly somewhere our Rex would fit in. What is the assignment?"

"It relates to that skirmish in Eastern Thrace last month. I presume you know the one I mean?"

"Of course. I read about it in the papers. Seems we narrowly avoided causing another war. I can hardly believe anyone would consider fighting again, particularly given we're still grieving those we lost a few years ago."

"I quite agree," Audley said. "Most of us had little appetite for war against the Turks, even if the Greeks are our allies. I was most pleased when the Canadian Parliament refused to take up the matter for consideration. They pulled the wind from Lloyd George's sails. He had little choice but to allow the Turks and Greeks to negotiate their own settlement. The old blowhard is still seething, but at least we are safe enough from armed conflict. For the moment, anyway."

Dora nodded her head, but halted after a moment. "If you are happy with the outcome, why are you so stressed?"

Audley rifled through his papers until he found the one he needed. He handed it to Dora and explained, "Someone was feeding Lloyd George's cabinet false information, suggesting the Turks planned to ally with the Soviets. It was fuel for Lloyd George's fire and nearly led us into an utter catastrophe. I know who passed along the rumour. My problem, in short, is that I have yet to identify the why."

Dora skimmed over the page. It was minutes from an advisory meeting, with several mentions of the Soviets. She glanced up to meet Audley's gaze. "How can that be? Your spy network is second to none, even out-performing the new top-secret government department."

"The fact that you are aware of the existence of said department is proof of that," Audley agreed. "You now understand why this is fast becoming a source of serious consternation for me. In the heat of the moment, I had to focus my attention on getting the Canadians to act as they did. Now, I'm chasing a cold trail. Lord Rex can't do any worse than we've done so far. What say you? Is he fit for the task?"

Dora didn't rush to answer. Lord Audley would expect her to give the matter careful consideration. There was no doubt in her mind that manoeuvring around the halls of Parliament would be a somewhat familiar environment for Rex. Although neither he nor anyone in his family had a reputation for being an active member of government, Rex would certainly know the names and faces of the men he'd see there.

If anything, the lack of a known political affiliation would be to Rex's advantage. He could rub shoulders with men of both conservative and liberal bent, feigning interest in learning about more of their viewpoint.

The more she thought about it, the better she liked the suggestion. She would say yes, but with one condition.

"He can do it, but we can't throw him straight into the deep. Either you or I will have to accompany him, at least while he finds his feet."

Audley rubbed his chin. "How would that work? If Rex is to learn anything, he can hardly be seen as my man."

"You don't need to stick by his side forever. But surely, as his former commanding officer, you could find it in your heart to provide him with an introduction to the key players?" Dora fluttered her lashes, playing her role of femme fatale to the hilt. "Once he's made a few connections, it would only be natural for him to hire a secretary to assist him with his correspondence."

Audley laughed long and hard, longer than her vague attempt at humour was worth. Dora sensed it had little to do with her and everything to do with the stress weighing on his shoulders. She sat back and sipped her drink, letting him release the pent-up emotions from the previous weeks.

"As always, my dear Theodora, you've thought of every eventuality. I agree with your conditions and suggest we start as soon as Rex can be ready. Bring him here tomorrow evening and we'll hammer out the details."

Chapter 3
Rex drags his heels

R ex checked and double-checked the instructions on the note, fully expecting them to have changed since he first read them. If he hadn't recognised the handwriting as Inga's, he'd have assumed it was some kind of joke.

But no, the words hadn't floated off the page, or disappeared to reveal a hidden code underneath.

"Lord A is expecting you to pay a call at nine this evening. Don't be late, and use the front door."

Rex pulled a lighter from his pocket and lit the corner of the paper. A few seconds and one singed finger later, nothing remained but ashes. Rex wiped the ash from the seat of his Rolls Royce Silver Ghost with his handkerchief, checked his watch, and then exited the car.

The night was cool but clear, the rain and wind of the previous day having temporarily freed London from its heavy atmosphere of clouds and smoke. The moon and stars twinkled above, tempting man into dreaming of impossible futures. On nights such as this one, Rex sometimes settled onto the cushion of his window seat and gazed upward, wondering what it would be like to touch those stars. Man had learned to soar in the sky.

It wasn't impossible to believe he might one day go even farther afield.

Not that Rex had any desire to travel far from Earth. Simply being in Dora's aura was close enough to star power for him. That was, in fact, the source of his current consternation. The last time Audley had invited him to visit, he'd walked out an hour later as a newly minted spy trainee. This time, he worried it would be the exact opposite. He didn't need to read Dora's notes to know he couldn't get anything right. Perhaps tonight was the night Audley would call time on this strange experiment and send him packing.

The church bell tolled the first of nine bells, putting an end to Rex's reverie. He straightened his coat and crossed the street, trying desperately hard not to picture himself as a dead man walking. If Dora were here, she'd tell him to buck up and face whatever happened next with a confident smile and air of nonchalance.

Easy for her to say.

Still, something in that advice must have stuck because Rex picked up his pace and climbed the front steps. Audley's old butler answered the door with a dour expression on his face.

"Good evening, your lordship. Come in. Lord Audley is expecting you."

Rex handed his coat and hat to a housemaid, taking care to check that she wasn't Dora in disguise. The housemaid mistook his interest for something else and gaped a gap-toothed smile at him.

Rex grimaced at his error and twirled around to follow the butler to Audley's study.

Audley sat behind his monstrous wooden desk, an antique piece that had likely been in his family for centuries. Dora, resplendent despite her muted clothing of black and grey, waved her fingers in hello. She motioned for Rex to take the seat

18

beside her in one of the wooden chairs in front of the desk.
Despite the late hour and intimate location, the trio might as
well have been in a bank or law office.

Lord Audley's face betrayed nothing of his inner thoughts.
He folded his hands and rested them on top of the desk. "Lord
Rex, I'm pleased you could join us. Miss Laurent and I have
been discussing your progress and next steps. I understand you
have completed the training programme to her satisfaction.
Therefore, it is the appropriate time for you to take the next pass
forward."

Rex blinked a few times, sure he'd misheard. Of all the ways
he'd pictured this conversation going, this wasn't one of them.

Dora reached over and squeezed his arm. "It's time for your
first mission, darling! Isn't that the bee's knees?"

Bee's knees? More like angry hornets swarming in his
midsection. He was discovering that the only thing worse than
being sent home was the possibility of being sent out on his
own. He was, to put it mildly, terrified of royally screwing up.

"I, err, I don't understand. A mission? For me?" Rex
grimaced at how inane he sounded. "Of course, I'm happy to
help in any way that I can."

"Excellent," Audley said, preventing Rex from further
waffling. "Before I tell you more about what you'll be asked to
do, it's best I explain how I choose agents for their particular
assignments."

Rex forced his shoulders to relax. An explanation would be
much appreciated.

"As you may have heard, there is a newly formed
government unit tasked with gathering intelligence from foreign
entities. Born out of the war, they aim their efforts at infiltrating
troops and gangs and using covert tactics to steal code sheets
and plans. This is not the type of work my agents do. Instead,
my team operates at a much higher level, gathering tidbits of

information directly from the mouths of world leaders, or feeding messages to those in power. I don't expect all my agents to show the same chameleon-like skills as Theodora. In most cases, I prefer to put people exactly where they fit in. For a man like yourself, that would be society events, private clubs, —"

"And Parliament," Dora said, hurrying Audley along. "How do you feel about taking a turn through the world of politics?"

Lord Audley glared at Dora for stealing his thunder. "I don't need you to run for office, or start drafting new legislation for the House of Lords," Audley assured a nervous-looking Rex.

"Parliament? You want me to go undercover in Parliament?" Rex's eyes nearly crossed as he attempted and failed to picture that scenario. He'd be locked away for even attempting such a feat.

"I want you to go to Parliament as yourself, Rex," Audley clarified. "This is not an undercover assignment. Think of it more as high time you took an interest in the major issues affecting our country. Since neither your father nor brother have ever shown an interest in taking their seats in the House of Lords, it only makes sense for you to come to me, your wartime commander, and ask for an introduction."

Rex nodded at Audley's sage words. "That's why I came in tonight through the front door?"

"It is, indeed. However, don't expect much in the way of further assistance from me. Given my tenure as an advisor to the King and the Prime Minister's cabinet, my position on most matters is well known. While that allows me access to certain whisper networks, equally, it prevents me from taking part in others. As a bright-eyed newcomer with no known allegiances, you can gain entry into rooms where I am unwelcome."

Rex felt the tension drain from his neck and back. Walking the halls and glad-handing with the old men in power couldn't possibly be dangerous. If anything, this so-called assignment sounded more like a next stage in his training. No more slinking around in the shadows. Instead, it was a case of getting out into the world and listening to powerful men debate. It would be just like his days in the military. Easy peasy.

"I'll do it, sir. You'll be pleased to know I am familiar with the platforms of the major parties. It would take little effort for me to choose select aspects of each and use a professed interest in them to justify a slow approach to picking a side."

"Excellent idea, but don't be too hesitant. I need fewer questions asked and more opinions expressed. In fact, showing yourself as willing to do whatever it takes to get accepted would be best. You'll need to give the right people enough hope that you'll go their way that they'll invite into their inner sanctums. That's where you'll get the information I need. Urgently," Audley added.

Those hornets in Rex's stomach took flight again. He knew it sounded too good to be true. Even Dora's words of encouragement did little to avail his skyrocketing anxiety. An urgent assignment? What would Dora do in his shoes?

She'd leap head first into things and would, no doubt, end up not only swimming, but doing the backstroke.

As much as Rex wanted to be like Dora, he knew such an audacious goal was still miles away. He'd learned the hard way that failed missions resulted in death. If not his, then someone else close.

No, far better to be honest about his shortcomings than to bluster through and hope to outrun his enemies. He already knew that his best simply wasn't good enough.

"I hate to speak out of turn, but if the matter is so urgent, I'm sure there must be someone better placed than I am. I'm still wet behind the ears when it comes to spying."

"I've told you time and again, Rex," Dora said. "The only

way to truly learn is by doing. Lord Audley wouldn't put you in this role if he didn't think you were capable."

"She's right," Audley said. "I have exactly one other agent operating in Parliament, and thus far, he has come up short."

Rex gulped. "You want me to do what a seasoned operative could not?" He was sure he'd misheard.

Lord Audley didn't blink. "Yes."

Rex opened his mouth, but no words came out.

Dora rushed to fill the gap. "Lord Audley is making it sound worse than it is. Yes, he's had someone looking for the information he needs for the last few weeks. And yes, they haven't succeeded. However, that is because the agent has had to work undercover, restricting his movements to the shadows. Your approach will be the opposite. Neither of us expects you to crack this nut in a matter of minutes. Go in, take things slow, and see what you can learn. If you discover anything, we'll already be ahead. And besides, either Lord Audley or I will be with you most of the time."

Rex turned his head to stare at Dora. "You're going to Parliament? You — as in Theodora Laurent? How will that even work?"

Dora tossed her head back and laughed. "Theodora can gain access to most anywhere, but multiple visits to Parliament would tax even her abilities. I'd adopt a much less glamorous identity. For example, have you ever wanted to have a private secretary?"

Rex couldn't imagine Dora passing anywhere unnoticed, but then again, she had fooled him more than once. With her by his side, the job seemed slightly less monumental. Instead of surmounting Everest, all they wanted him to do was climb the Alps. In the winter. Without any gear or safety harness...

He nipped that train of thought in the bud before the

downward spiral sucked away what little remained of his sanity. He forced air into his lungs and bade his thoughts to slow down.

The expressions on Dora's and Lord Audley's faces didn't shift. This wasn't a practical joke. They truly thought him capable of rubbing shoulders with England's leaders and elbowing his way into secret conversations.

Yet, he couldn't bring himself to say yes without first addressing the elephant sitting on his chest.

"What happens when I make a mistake? Don't shower me with platitudes. You know as well as I that I still have much to learn."

"Nothing," Dora replied without missing a beat. "In our line of work, there is no such thing as abject failure. Go to Westminster. Make friends. Encourage them to take you into their confidence. Anything you learn will be useful, even if it might not seem like so at the time."

"She's right. While Theodora reigns as the unofficial queen of the social scene, I still need someone in politics. You are the best person for the job. Are you willing to do this, or not?"

An answer sprang to Rex's mind, but he forced himself to wait a moment before answering. Did he want this badly enough to agree despite his nagging doubts?

One glance at Dora's wide emerald eyes and he was lost. "Okay, I'm in. What do you need me to find out?"

"Tonight? Nothing. Tomorrow is soon enough. I'll arrange for Emanuel Murdoch, the original agent, to meet the two of you. He'll tell you everything he knows about the current matter and anything else that might be of use. For now, I suggest we adjourn this portion of our evening and enjoy a drink instead. It's not often we welcome a new agent into the fold. The occasion warrants us raising our glasses in a toast."

Audley invited Dora and Rex to join him in his sitting room, where he'd taken the liberty of putting a bottle of Veuve Clicquot on ice.

Rex went through the motions of taking the proffered glass and raising it high. However, Lord Audley's toast fell on deaf ears. No matter what Audley said, Rex knew the truth. He had to succeed. If he didn't, the next thing they'd be toasting was his good riddance.

Chapter 4
The missed meeting

D ora eyed the stack of magazines on her desk. They were an eclectic mix of fashion titles, gossip rags, and political think-pieces. She felt an almost overwhelming urge to hide the most frivolous of titles, before ultimately deciding to leave them exactly where they were. The irony of her quandary wasn't lost on her. Of all the rooms in her spacious home, her study was the most private.

Tucked away at the rear of the house, the architect hid the only access point behind a bookshelf in the library. Unlike the front rooms, which were designed to convey everything anyone needed to know about Theodora Laurent, the study was for Dora.

The real Dora.

Even Inga and Harris were hesitant to tread over the threshold without an explicit invitation.

Although Dora had grown up in a stately manor house with a veritable surplus of spare bedrooms, she'd had little privacy. Housemaids came and went, and her brothers regularly invaded her space. She'd had to resort to finding hiding spots for her personal items.

Here, she was free to fill the bookshelves with her favourite stories without worrying they'd wander off. Instead of the works of sleek geometric shapes and the Japanese prints that graced her drawing-room walls, she had roughly drawn charcoal caricatures of her and Inga and a collage of postcards. Everywhere she looked, there was something to evoke a fond memory of her travels around the world.

Today, she was going to let Rex come inside the study. If anyone asked, Dora would have said that it was a simple precaution to keep prying eyes from seeing them talking for so long. The truth was much less easy to convey. She was fond of Rex. Moreover, despite what he thought, she saw much of herself in him. Like her, he shared her struggles to find a place in the world where he mattered.

Never mind that she was miles ahead of him. They walked along the same road.

If she wanted Rex to understand this, she had to reveal something of her hidden self. There was no more appropriate place to do that than here, in this secret room.

She'd left the bookshelf door ajar so she heard the exact moment Rex arrived. He knocked at the front entrance, playing his role of current suitor to the hilt, and came in with a bright hello for Harris and Inga.

It was the latter who accompanied him to Dora's study. Inga stuck her brunette head through the open doorway and asked, "You want to come out?"

"No, but thanks for checking. Please send Rex in."

Inga's wide-eyed stare had Dora second-guessing her decision, but Rex was over the threshold before she finished her thought.

To give him credit where credit was due, Rex approached the hidden room with a suitable level of awe. He remained silent while scanning the contents of the room, although he broke a smile at the charcoal drawings.

Dora shifted in her chair, having the uncomfortable sensation that her underwear were on display. That, however, would have been easier to manage. She knew what to do when wearing only her unmentionables in front of a man. Inviting him into her inner sanctum was a different matter.

Rex ventured closer to the caricatures. "Where are these from?"

"Paris. It was our first trip together. After months spent nursing on the front lines, wandering carefree over the bridges of the Seine felt more dream-like than reality. A street artist called us to come closer. I'd have said no, but it was clear from the bandages on his legs that he'd seen action. We let him draw us and then I paid him thrice what he asked."

"Worth every penny," Rex said. "He captured your doe-like eyes perfectly. When you flutter your lashes, every other feature on your face practically disappears." He grinned at her to let her know he was poking fun.

Just like that, Dora's nerves settled, and she remembered why she'd chosen to have their conversation here. She rose from her desk and pointed to the small seating area. "Please, have a seat."

Rex chose the chair nearest the door, leaving Dora the other. Dora poured two cups of tea from the pot on the table and passed one to Rex.

"Although I'm sure the hidden doorway makes the private nature of this room self-evident, there is a reason I wanted you to see it today."

Rex glanced around. "Will I need a secret room?"

"No, this isn't going to be a conversation about real estate. I need to talk to you about identity."

"I see..." he said, even though he didn't see at all.

Dora set her teacup aside and leaned forward. "I'm making a hash of this. Let me start again. Sometime in the next few days, you'll accompany Lord Audley to the House of Lords. There, you'll spin the first threads in the web of lies that will become your spy cover. It was the same for me when I took that first trip to Paris with Inga. We bought new clothes, ate good food, slept — basically enjoyed all the luxuries we'd given up when we signed on as nurses. We didn't do those things out of vanity. We did them because we had to do so, especially if we wanted the world to believe we were women of independent wealth with vague backgrounds."

This time, Rex opted for honesty. "I don't understand."

"Every time I set foot outside this house, I am playing the role of Theodora Laurent. After a night out on the town, I come back here, to this room, and remember who I am. Who Dora is — not Theodora Laurent. Dora is a daughter, sister, nurse, and friend. She isn't some brazen vixen out on the prowl. Dora likes serialised novels, fashion magazines..."

"And politics," Rex added, thumbing at a nearby newspaper open to the political section.

"Well, yes. There is some overlap between me and my alter-ego. That's what makes it possible for me to play her as well as I do. Consider this your final lesson, if it makes it easier. Where does Rex — dutiful grandson, dedicated friend, and lover of fast cars — end and where does your Lord Rex identity begins."

Rex creased his brow. "In my case, aren't they one and the same?"

"Right now, yes. But in a couple of week's time when you've told a lie here and there, professed an interest in something you hate... then, you'll notice a gap between your two personas. Showing you this secret room of mine was the best way to illustrate my point."

Dora watched as Rex cocked his head to the side. Based on his serious expression, she'd got through to him.

"It helps if you take a couple of trusted people into your confidence. I've got Inga and Harris. They know everything there is to know about who I am. In your case, I'd suggest you start with your grandmama."

"I can do better than that. There's her, you, Inga and Harris, the twins... and unless you strongly disagree, I'd like to bring my valet into the group."

"I don't disagree at all. His assistance will come in handy should you ever need to don clothes not appropriate for your station. One last thing, before we go. From today, you have an open invitation to visit this room anytime you need a safe place to get your head on straight."

Rex's mouth dropped open. "I couldn't... I mean, this is yours!"

"I didn't say you should move in and leave your things everywhere!" Dora replied, shaking her head. "You silly man, you know what I am saying. This is a sanctuary from spy life. Treat it with respect and we'll be fine. Now, get your coat. We've got an appointment to keep."

Dora stood, and Rex copied her motions. However, when she went to slide past him, he put out a hand and stopped her.

His fingers rested lightly on her waist, yet still somehow managed to burn an imprint on her skin. He tilted his head down so he looked her in the eye. In a voice barely louder than a whisper, he said, "Thank you. For this, for all the training, for sharing your friends with me, for everything."

Dora flattened her hands against his chest and rose on her toes and kissed him on the cheek. "You're welcome. I mean it. You are *always* welcome."

Dora smoothed the front of his shirt and then stepped back to give him a critical eye. "This linen is far too fine. Let me ask

Harris to find you something more akin to the middle class than the upper crust before we head out. We're meeting Murdoch at his flat."

Harris did indeed have something suitable in his wardrobe, although the fit wasn't exactly right. When Rex pointed that out, Harris told him in no uncertain tone that such problems were normal when one couldn't afford to have everything they owned custom-tailored to their exact measurements.

Dora overheard the exchange and had to bite the inside of her cheek to keep from laughing out loud. Poor, dear Rex. He'd made such progress, but still had a way to go before they rubbed all the shine off of him.

"If you think the clothing is bad news, I'm about to make it worse," she informed Rex on their way out the door. "We're taking the Model T."

Rex kept walking, feigning indifference. "At least promise me you aren't driving."

"Harris will have that honour," Dora replied. "With his cap on and you and I in the back, it will look as though we're in a taxi."

It took them nearly half an hour to crawl through the traffic to reach Murdoch's rented accommodations. Dora kept up a steady chatter for the first fifteen minutes of it, but she soon sensed that Rex wasn't paying her full attention. Likely, he was busy thinking about what she'd told him, and how that might affect his coming days.

Murdoch's flat was in a Victorian-era boarding house, a stone's throw from Westminster. Dora and Rex strode through the front door without encountering anyone else. Number thirty-eight was on the third floor up, at the far end of the corridor. Based on the location of the door, Dora guessed it looked onto the rear courtyard.

She decided then that she approved of this Murdoch.

Anonymous housing with plenty of other residents meant few would note his comings and goings. While the rear flats likely had little view, they had the advantage of being quieter.

The hallway was silent. Dora's light rap on his door echoed off the wooden floor, but elicited no reply. She tried again.

"Are we early?" Rex mumbled.

"Late. I make it a point to always arrive a few minutes past when I'm expected." Dora raised her voice. "Mr Murdoch? It's me, Theodora."

"Maybe we got the meeting place wrong," Rex said, but stopped speaking when Dora glared at him.

"Drat that man," she grumbled. Although she had little hope, she decided to try the door handle. It twisted smoothly under her hand. She pushed it open and stuck her head in to call another greeting.

That was as far as she got.

Instead of finding the expected mix of cheap furniture in bland colours, she saw total disarray. Dora pushed the door open wider and strode inside, pulling Rex in with her. "Close the door," she ordered when he froze in place.

Rex pushed the door shut with his heel, stunned by the sight of loose papers, shredded upholstery, and ripped books flung about the place. He leaned over to retrieve a sofa cushion from the floor, but Dora stopped him.

"Don't touch anything," she hissed. She picked her way between the chaos, aiming for the doorway on the other side of the sitting room.

Rex, at a loss for what else to do, followed her, taking care to step where she'd done. He was so busy looking down that he didn't glance up again until they entered the bedroom and she shuffled sideways.

That left a clear view for both of them to see the blood

sprayed across the white bedspread and dotting the wall. There was no sign of their missing agent.

Rex stumbled backward. Dora thrust out a hand to catch him.

"Where are you going?"

Rex's face was white. He gave a choked cry and gasped for air.

"Oh no, you don't." Dora spun him around and pushed him into the sitting room. "Go crack that window open and breathe the fresh air. I'll be back in a second."

"Back?" Rex paled further and swayed.

"Yes. I will be back," she assured him in the no-nonsense tone mothers reserved for mischievous children. "We need the help of a professional."

Rex gulped. However, between the steadying tone and reassuring promise of help, his face pinked up a shade. "Will you telephone the police?"

"I'll do one better. I'm going to get Harris."

Chapter 5
A butler's work is never done

Rex took deep breaths at the sitting-room window, with his eyes firmly fixed on the plain brick facade of the building behind. How could Dora be so sanguine about what they'd seen?

Blood stains shouldn't bother a man with his wartime experience. But it was one thing to see crimson on the battlefield, and another to come across it in a home. Those bright stains had caught him off guard and slipped past all his defences, catapulting him back to a place where he felt in constant fear for his life.

He panicked for a second when the door handle turned, but it was only Dora, accompanied by Harris as promised.

Harris whistled when he got a good view the room. "It was like this when you came in?"

"We didn't touch anything," Dora assured him. "I had a quick glance in the room, but didn't see any sign of a body. I didn't want to risk overlooking a clue. What do you want us to do?"

"For now, go keep his lordship company there by the window while I size the situation. Then, we'll talk."

Lynn Morrison

Dora picked her way across the room, dancing around the piles of cushion stuffing and book spines. She did it so naturally that she might as well have been spinning around a ballroom. Rex tried to take comfort from her grace, but set against the stark disarray of the room, it was nigh impossible.

Dora finally reached his side and laid a hand on his upper arm, rubbing soothing strokes up and down its length. "There now, it will all be fine. Harris is here, and he's absolutely brilliant in situations like this one. In fact, I posit that there's no one better."

Rex turned to scrutinise her expression, unable to believe his ears. "Dora, one's butler is meant to be capable of handling most any situation, but surely making sense of the scene of a violent crime is beyond any butler's abilities."

Dora's mouth spread into a sly grin. "That's only because most people don't hire ex-detectives to work in their household."

"Ex-detective?" Once again, Rex repeated Dora's last words. "Harris was a detective?"

"Yes, didn't we tell you? I met Harris at a scene not wildly different from this one, although it was at a seaside hotel and not a boarding house. I was on the hunt for a double agent and my prime suspect wound up dead. Harris was ready to throw me in the clink until Inga convinced him of my innocence. His interest in her took an amorous turn, and before I knew it, they had fallen in love. When it was time for us to go, Inga issued an ultimatum. Harris didn't have to think twice. After all, he is still in His Majesty's service, albeit in a somewhat different capacity. So there you have it!"

Dora's quick summation left Rex with more questions than answers, but a loud thud followed by a sharp gasp cut him off.

"Harris?" Dora asked, her voice pitched high with worry.

"I'm all right," he replied, although his tone conveyed anything but that.

Footsteps proceeded the man's return to the sitting room. He was in one piece, but there was a fresh splotch of blood on his sleeve.

"Bad news. Your agent isn't missing. I found him stuffed inside the wardrobe. It's Murdoch all right. His identification was in his pocket. The body's still warm. My best guess is that you missed the intruder by less than an hour."

Rex felt a tremor run along his spine. "If we'd met here instead of me coming to yours, we might have been able to save him."

"Or," Dora posited, "We might be lying beside him. That way lies madness, darling, so I suggest you abandon that path at its start." She patted him on the shoulder and turned to speak with Harris. "What do you make of the rest of this? Did he surprise a thief?"

Harris crossed back to the main door and examined the handle and the door frame. Then, he opened the door and checked the outside. Satisfied with what he'd learned, he assessed the chaos in the flat.

"There's no sign of forced entry. Despite the disorder, there's also no sign of a fight. Here's my take... Murdoch invited his killer inside. He must have gone into the bedroom for something. The killer followed and slit his throat. That accounts for the blood on the bed. Whoever it was, they had enough strength to manoeuvre the body into the wardrobe. With Murdoch out of the way, the killer spent the remaining time tossing the place."

Rex was awestruck by the concise explanation of the scene. Hearing it explained so logically helped him overcome the last of his nausea and focus on what Harris was saying. He wasn't about to venture back into the bedroom, but here, by the window, he felt safe enough.

"Do you think they were searching for something?" Rex asked.

"Examine the scene, mate," Harris answered. "Seriously. It's rare to get a training opportunity such as this one. We should make the most of it."

Rex wanted to argue that the dead man in the other room might disagree, but with both Harris and Dora staring at him expectantly, he sensed it was a losing battle. He forced himself to step away from the window and to examine the strewn mess on the floor.

"Don't think about where things are now," Harris added. "Imagine how the room would have looked before all this happened."

That was easier said than done, but the exercise put Rex even more on firm ground. He let his gaze skim the room. There was a sofa and armchair, a narrow bookshelf running from floor to ceiling, a table with two chairs, and a kitchenette with a single gas burner and a sink.

The kitchen cupboards were still closed, their contents seemingly untouched, although he'd have to check to be sure. Rex mentally gathered all the loose stuffing from the floor and put it back into the sofa and chair cushions. Next, he imagined himself shelving the books. There were only enough there to fill half of the shelves. That left only the loose papers, folders, and envelopes.

"Got the picture in your head?" Harris asked and waited for Rex to nod in confirmation. "Excellent. Now walk me through the perpetrator's actions."

That made sense. Rex used the toe of his shoe to slide a book over, revealing the edge of the paper underneath. He recognised the symbol stamped onto the page. The emblem of the portcullis with the crown on the top emblazoned across the top proclaimed them to be official parliamentary documents.

Murdoch had brought some of his work home with him.

"The intruder went through Murdoch's papers before they did the bulk of the damage," Rex said.

Harris and Dora rewarded him with matching expressions of satisfaction.

Harris clapped his hands. "Well done. Now answer me this. Was the perpetrator searching for something, or attempting to make this look like a robbery gone wrong?"

"I, err, that is..." Rex quieted while surveying the room again. He desperately wanted to give the right answer, but he didn't have a clue. Well, it was a fifty-fifty shot. "Searching for something?"

Dora's smile collapsed into a frown, and Rex knew he'd got that one wrong. Darned if he knew why, however.

"I can't say with one hundred per cent certainty, but my gut instinct is no. Shall I tell you how I know?" Harris asked.

Rex nodded.

"They only tossed this room, and not the other one. They shoved the clothes to the side in the wardrobe and the drawer in the bedside table was closed. That's my first clue. The second one is the fact that they weren't here when you arrived. To me, that says they tossed things around and then beat a path out the door."

"And with it being a weekend, chances of anyone else taking note of who came through are nigh impossible," Dora groaned.

"Shouldn't we ask around? We could canvas the floors," Rex argued.

"We can't." Harris's tone left no room for argument. "We'd have to offer some sort of explanation for our questions, and that would only lead to further trouble. When a man dies in the line of duty — spy duty, that is — we hush up the investigation and solve it in secret. Audley will know if Murdoch has any surviving family. He'll see the man buried and care for any family remaining. What we won't be doing is telling anyone outside our inner circle that Murdoch is dead."

"But—" Rex stammered.

"He's right," Dora said. She shrugged her shoulders and frowned in consternation. "Even the best police investigator in the world is going to struggle to solve a crime where the motive is top secret. This is exactly why Audley approved of me bringing Harris onto the payroll."

Rex slumped in defeat and huffed out a breath. "You're right, but it feels as though we're dumping this problem in Harris's lap."

Harris's eyes widened, and he barked a laugh.

Dora frowned him into silence and then broke the bad news to Rex. "Harris will do his part. We all will," she stressed. "But the heavy-lifting of this assignment is going to fall squarely on your shoulders. On our shoulders," she hurried to correct. "Without leaping to conclusions, it does seem likely we'll find the identity of our murderer by exploring Parliament and not London's back alleys."

Rex feverishly shook his head. "On no. Not again. It was bad enough I ended up involved in finding Freddie's killer. I never meant for that to be more than a one-off."

"A two-off." Dora wiggled her eyebrows. "You've solved two murders, if you count the one we solved during the war. After two cases, I'd say we're old hands at this."

"More qualified than the average officer on the street," Harris added.

Rex was still shaking his head. "This time is different. If we continue with my mission as planned, I'll be stepping right into the line of fire, and taking you and Lord Audley with me." Rex pleaded with the pair to understand. He didn't know how Dora and Harris had overlooked this fact, but he wasn't going to sit quietly until the realisation struck.

Dora and Harris exchanged weighty glances, having an entire conversation without saying a word.

Harris backed up a step, moving closer to the bedroom. "Tell you what, I'll leave you two to discuss while I finish checking the other room."

Dora took Rex's hands in hers and gave them a squeeze. Her smile was pained, but her emerald eyes were kind. "This is hard. You're right to say this isn't the same as last time. Then, you took it upon yourself to find Freddie's killer. He was your dear friend, and that was all the incentive you needed. This time, you believe you can walk away because it is a stranger. This logic fails to account for one key aspect."

"What's that?"

"Your country needs you. I make this whole spy thing seem like fun and games, but that's to keep the sheer seriousness of our task from overwhelming us. None of us want a repeat of the war unless it absolutely cannot be avoided. The work we do enables Lord Audley and the other leaders to make informed decisions about challenges we face. Murdoch understood this. As far as I'm concerned, we owe it to him to finish his work and, if possible, identify his killer. Because as bad as this looks, if we stop our efforts now, the situation is likely to get even worse."

Dora spread their hands wide and stepped into the gap, closing the distance between them. "Do you know that you wear your thoughts across your face? I can see that you have doubts. That is human! But I believe in you. We all do, Rex. What I'm asking is for you to stay the course on this mission."

Rex stared down into the pools of her eyes. For once, however, he wasn't seeing the green depths. Instead, he saw the quick, sure strokes of a piece of charcoal in an artist's hand. Theodora Laurent was more than capable of manipulating a man into doing her bidding. This time was different.

Dora was speaking from her heart.

Rex inclined his head in a single nod of agreement. "Tell me how we do this, and above all, promise me we'll do it together."

"That is an assurance I can give, and give again. No matter what happens, you are part of a team now. John Donne said it best." Dora closed her eyes and recited from memory,

"'No man is an island entire of itself; every man is a piece of the continent, a part of the main; if a clod be washed away by the sea, Europe is the less, as well as if a promontory were, as well as any manner of thy friends or of thine own were; any man's death diminishes me, because I am involved in mankind. And therefore never send to know for whom the bell tolls; it tolls for thee.' Today, the bell tolls for Murdoch, and for us. We will honour him by answering the clarion call to finish his mission."

Rex had all but forgotten Donne's famous words. Hearing them now, in Dora's feminine voice, they took on greater meaning than ever before. "Where do we start?"

"At my home. Gather all the papers you can and we'll carry them with us. I'll send Archie and Basil back to assist Harris with removing the body and securing the flat. Between my political insights and Inga's cool logic, I'm sure we can assemble the first pieces in this puzzle."

Chapter 6
The history lesson

Dora and Rex marched through her front door, arms laden with documents and files. She shouted for Inga to pull the dining room curtains wide open to allow sunlight to illuminate the room. While Inga got to work clearing the floral arrangements from the centre of the table, Dora updated Archie and Basil on their assignment to assist Harris back at the scene of the crime.

With the twin footmen on their way out the door, Dora and Rex dropped their stacks onto the table and asked Inga to help. The trio got to work on sorting the mountain of papers into some semblance of order. In short order, Dora's dining room table was almost completely obscured by papers.

An upper class dining room could be expected to play host to any number of occasions. However, Dora doubted the designer of her custom table had murder investigations in mind when he'd paired the heritage oak top with the lacquered, x-shaped metal base. Although, to be honest, it looked more like the office of a dedicated MP than the workplace of a police officer.

The contents were as varied as the handwritten notes in

their margins. There were official proclamations, drafts of private bills, speeches, meeting minutes, and even the hastily scrawled dinner order from a meeting stretched long. Still, Dora didn't let the volume of papers stand in her way of making heads or tails of their content.

She made a full lap around the twelve-person table, picking up a paper here and there to examine more closely. When she was done, she waited for Inga to finish doing the same. When Inga halted opposite her, their eyes met over the top of the table.

"Everything I saw related to that affair in Eastern Thrace. Did you find the same?" Inga asked.

"Yes, not that it was a surprise, given what Lord Audley had told me about Murdoch's assignment."

Rex waved a hand to get the women's attention. "Eastern Thrace? Are you referring to the recent incident in Chanak, by any chance?"

"You know of it?" Dora asked.

"I saw the headlines." Rex shifted awkwardly. "I suppose now would be a good time to admit that I didn't commit the details to memory. I've had my mind on the training exercises."

Dora circled the table and gave him a quick squeeze of assurance. "We don't expect you to do it all, darling. Why do you think I have a team? Over time, you'll figure out what areas of expertise interest you the most, and which ones you prefer to delegate to someone else."

"If I may?" Inga interjected. "Dora is correct in one aspect. The team works best when everyone's assignments align with their interests. However, she left out that other part, which is that each team member should bear an equal share of responsibility for the dirty work."

"I think what Inga is trying to say is that while we may lead by example, we gain loyalty by pushing up our sleeves. Right now, we will do just that. Why don't we all take a seat and Inga and I can fill in the gaps of your understanding of the situation?"

Rex and Inga pulled out chairs from the table while Dora rang the bell for the housemaid. She was the newest member of the household, a young woman of eighteen. She also happened to be the younger sister of Archie and Basil.

"Cynthia, would you mind bringing us a pot of tea and a plate of sandwiches?" Dora asked when Cynthia appeared in the dining room doorway.

Cynthia bobbed her dark head and rushed to do her mistress's bidding.

"Now that refreshments are en route, where should we start? Inga, do you want to go first?"

"And have you interrupt me every time I leave something out?" Inga shook her head. "No, I'll let you start."

"In that case, I'll make doubly sure to be comprehensive for fear of you doing the same," Dora quipped back. "Believe it or not, our problems started a little over a month ago in the Aegean. The Turks, under the leadership of Mustafa Kemal, were determined to regain their capital city of Constantinople. As that area lay in the neutral zone between Turkey and Greece, their advancement brought them into firm opposition with our troops. I shouldn't side with our opponent, but Kemal was most reasonable. While willing to fight, he said he preferred negotiation rather than war."

"Given the time all three of us spent on the front lines, I can certainly understand your sentiments," Rex agreed. "And we didn't go to war, so I can only assume said negotiation took place."

"It did, and in fact finished only a couple of days ago, with the signing of an armistice." Dora leaned over and lifted one of the documents from the table. "This appears to be an early draft of the text."

Rex skimmed the document and then passed it along to Inga. "If the matter is settled, why kill Murdoch? In fact, why was Murdoch involved?"

Before Dora could reply, Cynthia returned with a tray of tea and plates of sandwiches. The team carefully cleared space on the table and distributed the drinks and food before returning to the conversation.

Dora washed down a finger sandwich with a sip of tea and recommenced. "Now that you know this story has a happy ending, at least in terms of avoiding risk to life and limb, I will tell you what happened behind the scenes. It may surprise you to learn that Lloyd George was far more willing to take up arms against the Turks, arguing it was our duty to aid Greece to retain their hold on the territory. He might have won the day if two countries hadn't refused to comply. The first was France. The second was Canada."

"Canada?" Rex goggled. "But Canada is a dominion of the United Kingdom. We share the same king."

"Yes, but unlike during the Great War, our esteemed colleagues in Canada did not agree to blindly follow our lead into battle."

Rex was still shaking his head. "That makes little sense! What you're suggesting is a monumental change in their relationship with England. Setting aside the rightness of the outcome, I can't imagine how their Prime Minister would have dared to take such an action."

"And with that, we arrive at the point where Lord Audley comes into the discussion."

Rex choked on his tea. After spluttering for a second, he regained control and said, "Lord Audley, our Audley, encouraged the Canadian Prime Minister to go against the wishes of the British Prime Minister?"

Inga stifled a laugh and handed Rex a napkin. "Any port in a

44

storm, Lord Rex. Believe me, he's done far more outrageous things in the past few years. If anything, I consider this particular outreach to be tame."

"Now, Inga," Dora intervened. "You're going to scare Rex away before he gets settled into the role."

Inga flattened her lips and glared at Dora. "I'm fairly certain the dead body did more damage than anything I could say."

Rex flinched.

His movement caught Dora's attention. She was at risk of losing him down the rabbit hole of worry if she didn't get the conversation back on track.

"Let's return to the matter at hand. As I was saying, England was on the precipice of war with Turkey. Lloyd George's cabinet was split on the matter. To prevent tragedy, Lord Audley spoke with the Canadian Prime Minister. He dragged his heels on coming to England's aid."

Rex raised a hand, earning a laugh from Dora. "Why was the cabinet split? I still don't understand why some men in power were so keen to take on the Turks, especially given their stated willingness to negotiate."

"And now for the crux of the matter," Dora replied. "What if I told you that the Soviets were secretly supporting the Turks? By bowing down to the Turkish demands, the government could be opening itself up to further losses to the communists."

Rex paled. "That would change things. Until now, I'd been in agreement with Lord Audley's moves. Given our country's current challenges with those who aspire to a communist England, I'm right back on unsteady ground." He stopped to rub his temples. "Forgive me, but this is beginning to sound like a fictional tale used to challenge university students during their exams. All possible answers are both right and wrong, depending on where you decide to stand on the matter."

Dora flourished her hands. "Welcome to the world of

politics, Rex. Since this isn't an exam, I'll give you one more clue to help guide you to the right outcome. The intelligence suggesting the Russian-Turkish alliance was a lie."

Rex rocked back in stunned silence. "Blood, err, bother. This story gets worse with every turn."

"Lucky for you, we're at the end. The papers conveyed how the matter was resolved. France refused to agree to war. Canada absented themselves from the discussions. Lloyd George was forced to agree to a negotiated peace that returned Constantinople to the Turks. The coalition government remains on unsteady feet, but that isn't our problem, nor was it Murdoch's. Instead, Audley needs our help to identify why someone initiated the false rumours of the Soviet involvement in the matter."

"That's the information Murdoch was after?" Rex asked.

Dora nodded. "Yes. We know who passed the rumour along to Lloyd George. It was a member of his own party, one Lord St Cecil."

"The name rings a bell, but I cannot attest to knowing the man well."

"Then allow me to enlighten you. St Cecil is part of a cohort of eminent statesmen who act as advisors to the Government. All are peers of the realm with extensive experience in their areas of expertise. Lord Audley is one and is the only non-partisan member of the group. Of the remaining members, there are three Conservatives, two Liberals like Lloyd George, and two who side with the Labour party."

Rex steepled his fingers. "If Audley knew St Cecil was behind the rumour, why didn't he ask the man straight out?"

"He did. St Cecil claimed to have received the information from an unimpeachable source and refused to say more than that. Lloyd George, ever keen to fight the Turks, put a stop to any further discussions on the matter. He took the information and ran with it for as long as he could."

"I still don't get it — why didn't Lord Audley take St Cecil at his word? Is it that hard to believe the man might have insider information?"

Dora started shaking her head before Rex finished his question. "Problem was, St Cecil's area of expertise is not in foreign affairs. He is an economist, with a specific interest in rebuilding our post-war economy. Audley couldn't figure out why St Cecil suddenly proclaimed to have insights into Russian activities. The man detests the communists, for goodness' sake! Even once the rumour was proven to be false, St Cecil stuck to his guns. The man nearly caused us to go to war. For that alone, Audley needs to understand why St Cecil is still hiding his source."

Rex nodded. "I think I understand, although it is hard to believe a prominent lord would want to destabilise the country."

"If you ask me," Inga said, offering her opinion, "St Cecil was either someone's stooge, and is too embarrassed to admit it, or he lied for his own gain. Problem is, we don't have evidence to tell us which one it was."

"Is that what Murdoch was doing?" Rex glanced between Dora and Inga. "Was he investigating St Cecil?"

Dora responded to his question. "Yes. Audley recalled Murdoch from his latest assignment abroad. Audley then arranged for the agent to work in Westminster as a staff member. This gave Murdoch access to files and private papers, as you can see," Dora added, waving to the stack of documents. "As far as Audley knew, Murdoch wasn't having any luck. However, given our gruesome discovery, the evidence suggests otherwise. Murdoch must have been much closer than he realised. He did something to give away his interest and paid with his life. If we had any doubts that this is the work of a traitor, it is time to set them aside. If we don't find them, and put their meddling to a stop, I'm not exaggerating when I say that thousands of more lives might be at risk."

Dora didn't shift her gaze from Rex. She watched the lines of his shoulders and clocked the movement of his eyes. If he still had doubts about his fitness for the mission, she'd see it in his body language.

Rex held still, pondering her words and the implications. "Let me make sure that I've understood this right. Lord Audley wants me to uncover the motives of a potentially traitorous peer by networking?"

"I imagine it will entail more than raising a few glasses together. But surely you can see why you are the perfect person for this task. Who else could Audley send to match wits with prominent lords of the realm?"

After a moment of prolonged silence, Rex sat up straight, squared his shoulders, and looked down to check the time on his watch. "We've got hours left before bedtime. Hopefully that is long enough for you and Inga to tutor me on England's political leaders and the men and women working underneath them."

Dora didn't have to fake her smile. "I'll send a note to Lord Audley to tell him to prepare for your debut in the House of Lords. As for the rest, you can count on us."

Inga nodded her agreement. "After all the places we've been, papers we've read, and people we've met over the years, I can say one thing with certainty. Anything we can't teach you about political machinations isn't worth knowing."

Chapter 7
A visit to the House of Lords

Rex tugged at his bowtie, hoping in vain to loosen it enough for him to draw a full breath. Unfortunately, the silk tie wasn't the source of his trouble.

That honour went to the man sitting beside him in the back seat of the Rolls-Royce. Unlike Rex, Lord Audley was blithely unconcerned about their upcoming foray into the houses of Parliament.

Rex forced his hand down and willed his heart rate to follow suit. He was almost successful, but when the car turned the corner and Big Ben came into view, Rex gave up hope.

"Nervous, young man?" Lord Audley asked, casting Rex a side-eyed glance. His normally stern features relaxed enough to betray a smile.

"How could you tell?"

"Rex, I've seen men heading off to the trenches that looked more calm than you do now. You're visiting the House of Lords, not heading for a stay in the Tower. I'll start you off easy, introducing you to a few key people. All you have to do is pretend to be interested in what they're saying, not pry out their deepest, darkest secrets or sneak into their private files. Do try to keep that in mind."

Easy enough for Lord Audley to say. His head wouldn't be the one on the chopping block if Rex screwed something up.

Rex halted that line of thought. He wasn't being fair. Lord Audley was escorting him through the door, not pushing him off a proverbial cliff.

As though he were reading Rex's mind, Lord Audley chose that moment to reach over and give Rex and reassuring clap on the shoulder. "Chin up, Rex. You were born to this, and I mean that literally. While your immediate family may have chosen to spend their time elsewhere, plenty of the Bankes-Fernsby men have walked these same halls over the years."

"Were any of them spies?" Rex asked, sardonically. The only reply he got was Lord Audley's bland expression.

All too soon, the driver turned the car into the gap between the wrought-iron fence surrounding Parliament's majestic halls. The sand-coloured limestone shone gold under the sunlight. The gothic turrets and towers rose above the Georgian buildings in the surrounding neighbourhood. Even Westminster Cathedral, only a stone's throw away, failed to eclipse the breathtaking spectacle of Big Ben and the halls of government.

A uniformed guard waved the car through the gate and directed them to the Peers' Entrance located off the old palace garden. Rex cleared his mind of the last of his fears and prepared to exit the vehicle.

Thankfully, it wasn't Rex's first time setting foot within the Palace of Westminster. He'd visited a time or two during his school days, tagging along with other sons of the realm. As such, the encaustic tiles, panelled walls, soaring ceilings, and lines of towering paintings felt familiar enough that he avoided gawking like a newcomer.

Instead, he noted the way the people around them reacted to the arrival of Lord Audley.

The clerks present in the Peers' corridor scuttled out of the way as Lord Audley passed. They kept their gazes low and nodded at the vaunted statesman, almost as though they were bowing at the King. Rex had seen soldiers do the same whenever Audley had visited the front lines.

The Peers split themselves across three camps — those who despised Audley, those desperate to curry his favour, and the rare few who considered themselves to be equal to his station. It was a pair of men in the third category whom Audley approached.

The men stood near a painting commemorating the reign of William and Mary. Although they wore similarly cut Savile Row suits and silk ties, they couldn't have been more different. One stood a head taller than the crowd, while the other only came to his shoulder. What the second man lacked in height, he made up for with an impressive girth.

Lord Audley called out a greeting. "Morning, Harwich and Godfrey. I'd like to introduce you to Lord Reginald Bankes-Fernsby. His father is the Earl of Rockingham. Lord Reginald served under me at Le Touquet."

The men nodded their hellos to Rex. Lord Harwich, the taller of the pair, professed to know Rex's father from their school days. Lord Godfrey, however, was more curious to discover how Rex came to accompany Lord Audley.

"It isn't like you to act as a tour guide," Lord Godfrey commented, studying Lord Audley over the top of his pince-nez.

"That's my fault," Rex said, intervening before Audley found himself in the hot seat. "As you know, my father and brother have little interest in politics. I sent a note to Lord

Audley to ask if he'd do the honour of guiding me once again. To be honest, I had little hope of a yes."

"He caught me at a weak moment," Audley quipped. "Don't worry, gentleman. I assure you that doesn't happen more than once a decade."

As expected, the older men threw back their heads and laughed at the joke.

"I'd love to stand around and chat, but unlike some people who will remain unmentioned, my opinion is sought on sensitive matters. I don't suppose I could leave Lord Reginald in your capable hands?"

Rex blanched at the backhanded insult, but Audley's counterparts were long-since immune to his japes. Lord Godfrey stepped into the breech with an offer to host Rex for lunch in the Peers' dining room.

"Until then, I'll do my best to keep him out of trouble. And by trouble," Godfrey added, "I mean away from meddlers such as yourself, Audley."

Audley rolled his eyes and then clapped Rex on the back. "Do keep a closed mind around Godfrey and his fellow Tories. Although, listening to their party-line nonsense for a few hours might be just the trick needed to sway you to learn more about other viewpoints. See you later."

Harwich took the opportunity to make his excuses as well, leaving Rex alone with Lord Godfrey, one of the conservative members of the august group of peers. Somehow, Rex couldn't believe this was an accident, although he had no idea how Audley had accomplished it so handily. Either way, he would make the most of the opportunity.

"Lord Reginald.."

"Please, call me Rex. Even my mother doesn't use my full name," Rex said.

Lord Godfrey chuckled. "My given name is Barnabus, so

you have my sympathies. Tell me, Rex, what is it that has awakened your interest in political matters?"

Rex fell into step with the tall man. "You'll no doubt think me naive, but it was this recent matter with Turkey."

Lord Godfrey glanced sideways, with one eyebrow arched. "Are you a pacifist or are you bloodthirsty?"

Rex stumbled at the harsh question. "Err, neither? That is, I mean that, like so many others, I served on the front lines and witnessed the realities of war. While I have no great desire to return there, I am realistic enough to know that such sacrifices are, at times, required. That said, I was unsure whether the situation in Chanak rose to such a level of consideration. I'd be interested in hearing your opinion on the matter."

Lord Godfrey's expression shifted into one of exaggerated horror. "Egads, Lord Rex, you sound like Lord Audley when you waffle like that."

"Really?" Rex had not expected that statement. Audley had always struck him as incredibly decisive. He assessed and moved. The last sin Audley had was one of over-thinking. That was Rex's main problem.

Godfrey chuckled at Rex's chagrin. "Audley claims to be cross-bench, but I suspect he really thinks himself above the parties. Some days he sides with the Tories, others with the Liberals. One hundred per cent of the time, he justifies his position as being what is best for jolly old England. If you ask me, what's best is to put the reins in the hands of a like-minded group of individuals who can work together toward a shared outcome."

"I suppose you have a particular outcome in mind."

"Of course I do, my boy. After we make the rounds and say hello to a few chaps, we'll join my fellow Tories for luncheon. Unless, that is, you care to stake out a table in no-man's-land."

"That's hardly a safe position. Far better to sit in the

trenches with other fellows than strike out on your own. It remains to be seen whether I'll find myself with like-minded individuals or behind enemy lines."

At that remark, Lord Godfrey laughed and patted Rex on the back. "Good form, boy. I think you'll make an excellent politician."

Rex spent the remainder of the morning pondering that remark. He'd never given the political world a second thought, but now he wondered if he'd made a mistake. Although on the one hand, working for Lord Audley was, in essence, a political role, albeit a shadowy one. However, that wasn't to say he wasn't better suited for a life in the sunlight. If he took a seat in parliament, he wouldn't have to worry about picking locks or sneaking into buildings any longer.

However, he'd also lose his reason for staying close to Dora.

The question still weighed on his mind when Godfrey led him to a table for six in the Peers' Dining Hall. Between the ornate chandeliers, crisp, white linen tablecloths and polished silver, Rex might as well have been in one of London's finest dining establishments. The major difference was that there was nary a female in sight.

The long table sat in the corner of the room, and its occupants were deep in discussion. Rex recognised Lord Harwich from before, and Lord FitzClarence from his school days, but the rest were unknown. Likely, it was due to the age gap between himself and the older Lords. The war had put an end to socialising for a long stretch, curtailing even the societal introductions of the debutantes. After its end, society was slow to restart. Far too many were mourning their losses.

Rex's grandmother, the Dowager Duchess of Rockingham, did her best to cajole him into joining her at balls and dinners. Now, he wished he'd given in to more of her requests. If so, he'd be far more knowledgeable about the men around him. As it was, he'd have to depend on Lord Godfrey and his old school chum, Lord FitzClarence, to fill in the gaps.

After settling heavily into a chair, Lord Godfrey began. "Gentlemen, allow me to introduce Lord Rex of the Bankes-Fernsby family. Lord Rex, you know Lord Harwich already. The other men are Lords FitzClarence, Dorset, and Sutherland."

Rex nodded his head in greeting and took the proffered chair between Lord Sutherland and FitzClarence. Lord Sutherland, a distinguished gentleman with white hair and ruddy cheeks, paused only long enough to allow the server to take their orders before returning to a boisterous discussion about the pros and cons of a coalition government. Lord Godfrey was happy enough to take counterpoint to Sutherland's position.

While those two defended their positions on the matter, FitzClarence angled in Rex's direction and muttered under his breath, "How'd you get sucked into this world, Rex? I don't remember your family being active... nor conservative."

"I'm straying from the proverbial flock, Fitz. The only matter on which my father and brother have a firm opinion is the debate over which game should be eligible during hunting season."

Fitz chuckled under his breath. "Ahh, yes. They are both excellent shots, as I recall. Make sure you add my name to the list the next time you go up for a hunting weekend."

"Will do," Rex promised. The conversation ended abruptly when Godfrey mentioned Rex's interest in the Chanak Affair.

To a man, every individual at the table had an opinion on the matter. This time, they were in agreement.

"The idea of warring with the Turks was ludicrous, I tell you. For once, even the French got it right. Why Lloyd George and Churchill insisted on dragging out the discussion, I'll never know," Lord Dorset grumbled.

Lord Godfrey leaned over and replied in a low tone, "You heard what St Cecil said. They feared the Turks were considering an alliance with the Soviets."

"Poppycock!" Sutherland growled. "The Soviets are in no position to challenge us. Their people are starving, and they've barely put an end to their internal war."

"Be that as it may," Godfrey countered, "but they are awfully insistent on negotiating that union of theirs. Should they get the surrounding states to agree to a tight alliance, we'd be mad to ignore the risk they might pose."

Sutherland brushed Godfrey's remark aside. "I stand by my earlier statement. The fact that the Prime Minister and his esteemed colleagues consider the Russians a threat now is testament only to their unfitness to govern. That, my dear sirs, is a much more interesting discussion. I suggest we pick it up tomorrow."

Talk died down to more general matters while the men enjoyed a meal of beef Wellington and roasted potatoes. Rex grew so comfortable, he almost forgot why he was there.

It took a last word from his friend Fitz to drive home the reminder. "I say, Rex. I insist you come to a soiree at my home this evening. If you are looking for a chance to learn more about the political sides, I can assure you there'll be no shortage of peers at the event."

"I'd be delighted to attend."

"Excellent." Fitz beamed at him. "Do us all a favour."

At that remark, Rex grew wary. "Of course. What's that?"

Fitz wiggled his thick eyebrows. "Bring that new doll of yours, Miss Laurent. I'm desperate to make her acquaintance."

Rex tamped down his immediate reaction of jealousy and pasted a matching smile on his face. He wanted Dora by his side, and here was the perfect excuse to bring her along. Never mind that they weren't truly a couple. Surely Dora wouldn't take up with another man while pretending to be his paramour?

Rex pictured her sly grin and twinkling eyes and knew that when it came to Dora, absolutely anything was possible.

But he took great care not to let his true feelings show when he answered, "I'll have to check her diary, but if she hasn't other plans, I'd be happy to make the introduction."

Chapter 8
The pair attend a ball

Dora admired the two sets of matching jewellery lying on her dressing table. On the left was a platinum chain with an eye-catching diamond pendant accompanied by matching two carat earrings and a diamond bracelet. On the right, rectangle-cut rubies glowed in a deep red where they danced along the platinum chain. Based on her experience, once men got a look at the five-carat ruby drop nestled in her cleavage, they were willing to discuss most anything.

It was with great relief that she finally heard her bedroom door open and Inga's familiar footsteps clicking across her hardwood floor. "Oh good, you're here. Help me decide — fire or ice?"

"Given you're playing with fire, I would think the choice is self-evident."

Dora twisted on her stool to look at her dearest friend. "Whatever do you mean? I've been out with Rex dozens of times by now, and you've never raised an eyebrow."

"You've never accompanied him into the belly of the beast before."

Dora closed her compact with a snap. "I hardly think we

can equate a society soiree with spending three days in the belly of a whale."

"No? Then allow me to remind you of the risks you're taking." Inga lifted her hand to tick off each one. "First, Lord FitzClarence is a noted Tory. Second, your entire family is also notoriously conservative. Third, you haven't got anyone to cover for you should you run into them. Or does Lady Dorothy Cavendish expect her parents to let her waltz out the front door when they bump unexpectedly into their wayward child?"

Was that all? Dora turned back to her dressing table and lifted a puff to powder her nose. "The only Cavendish I'm likely to see is Benedict, and he already knows I'm here. My father hates these kinds of events and either avoids them entirely or spends the evening hiding in the game room playing cards."

Inga, however, refused to be put aside. "You forgot your mother."

"Mama, as you are very well aware, is at the country house. If that had changed, I'm sure Benedict would have found a way to get a message to me."

"Perhaps... but would Benedict expect you to turn up at a society ball? That's hardly your scene. But who I am to raise these points? It's your funeral."

"It's going to be yours if you don't help me pick a necklace." Dora swung around and stood so Inga got the full picture. With her hand propped on her hip and the devil-may-care gleam in her eyes, Dora fully embodied the exotic femme fatale identity known as Theodora Laurent. From the silken black plume on her sequinned headband to the plunging neckline and fringed hem of her skirt, Dora was simply stunning.

"Go with the diamonds."

"Really?" Dora lifted both necklaces and took turns dangling them around her neck.

"Absolutely. If you wear the rubies, poor Rex will end up so tongue-tied he won't be fit for sleuthing. Have pity on the man and put yourself on ice."

Cynthia knocked at the bedroom door and announced Rex's arrival before Dora came up with a suitable comeback. However, if the half-stunned expression on Rex's face when she came gliding down the stairs was any indication, the diamonds hadn't done nearly enough to lessen Dora's innate star power.

Harris gave Rex a helpful rap on the back to pull him from his state of reverie.

By then, Dora had reached the entryway. She spun in a circle, sending the beaded fringe on her skirt flying around her calves. "Will I do?"

"Too well," Rex replied. He helped her into her fur coat, letting his fingertips skim across the back of her neck. "When it comes to fisticuffs, please remember that you have no one to blame but yourself."

Dora rewarded his compliment with a saucy wink. "I've seen you boxing in the back garden with the boys. My money is going on you."

"Minx!"

Rex escorted her to the car, waiting until he'd pulled onto the road before updating her on his day.

"That's fantastic progress, darling!" Dora cooed when he finished his recount of lunch. "You say it was Lord Godfrey who brought up the rumour about the Russians? That puts him at the top of our list."

"I agree. My only regret was that due to his afternoon meetings, there wasn't more time for me to ply him with questions," he said. "But with you on my arm, I've no doubt that every man there will find an excuse to come over for a chat, Lord Godfrey included."

"A chat with me, you mean? But, darling, we need them to talk to you about politics, not whisper sweet words in my ear. I suggest we split up shortly after our arrival. You can head off to drink and smoke cigars with the men, which is where all the gossip is to be found, while I see what I can learn from those circling the ballroom."

Dora knew her plan was imminently sensible, but when Rex offered her his arm to escort her into the house, part of her wished they were there for fun. Sleuthing and spying always gave her a certain thrill, but having an exceptionally handsome man by her side held promises of its own.

Although she was far from a mere girl, she had found out the hard way not to mix business with pleasure. Right now, Rex was firmly planted in the business camp.

Someday, however, that might change. She'd be free to run her fingers through his blond hair, tousling the locks while he smothered her with kisses. Maybe once this current quest ended, when Rex wholeheartedly embraced the life of a secret spy, she would surrender to his touch.

She allowed herself a moment of weakness, leaning against his muscular form while they climbed the front stairs. But as soon as the front door swung open, revealing the receiving line waiting inside, Dora was firmly in control of all her emotions.

Rex guided her to their host. Lord FitzClarence was a dapper gentleman with a well-groomed moustache and a neatly trimmed goatee. He'd styled his auburn hair in a fashionable side parting, and his piercing brown eyes conveyed his intelligence. Like Rex, he was dressed in impeccable style. His custom-tailored evening dress included a white tie and tails.

Although there was a thin, gold band around his ring finger, his wife wasn't in the welcoming line.

"Perfect timing," Lord Fitz said, after bending over to kiss Dora's hand. "My wife was called away to resolve a matter with the housekeeper. That leaves me free to show you to the ballroom."

"I suppose I'm to make myself at home," Rex said with a sardonic grin. "Before you get your hopes up, I should warn you I have full faith in Miss Laurent's commitment to me."

"Of course you do," Fitz cried, laughing as though Rex had made an exceedingly clever joke. "Fear not, old friend. Her ladyship has a tight hold on my leading strings. Offering Miss Laurent my arm is as close as I'll come to infringing on your claim on her heart."

Dora knew she should play along, but her desire to keep everyone on their toes outweighed decorum. She grabbed a hold of Rex's lapels, tugged him close, and lifted on her toes to kiss him flat on the mouth. "Consider that a little something to keep you warm until you find me later on the dance floor."

Rex blushed so deeply that even the tips of his ears turned red.

Fitz, as he insisted Dora call him, made quick work of handing her furs off to a footman. He offered her his arm and led her into his home. It was a Georgian mansion with wings on either side of the front entrance. The ballroom lay in the wing on the right, past the dining room laid with a dazzling array of delicacies. Dora declined an offer of food and drink. She was more interested in tapping her toes to the live band.

"I do love to foxtrot," she purred while Fitz led her through the crowd of bejewelled guests. "Although, I had a man once tell me that watching me tango nearly brought him to his knees."

"Is that so?" Fitz gulped. "For that, you'll have to make a request to the bandleader. He's one of your countrymen, so that should give you an edge. The Claude Vidal Orchestra — are you familiar with them?"

"Claude is here?" Dora could hardly believe her ears. "Why didn't you say so from the start?"

With that, Dora tugged Fitz through the doorway into the ballroom. Couples of all ages twirled around the dance floor under the crystal chandeliers. The glass doors lining one wall reflected the lights and made the space look twice as big. The other wall was divided into arched alcoves, their entrances flanked by Doric columns topped with bronze urns. Hothouse flowers and cigarette smoke fought for dominance in the closed environs of the crowded room.

Dora, however, had eyes only for the skinny French man conducting the orchestra on the stage at the far end of the room. She immediately recognised the silvered hair and the way his hips swayed in time to the beat. It took all her restraint to wait until they finished their song before approaching the foot of the stage.

She marched through the dancers, clearing her own path, and stopped just shy of the stage. The lead trumpeter was the first to spy her. His dark eyes lit up in recognition, and he waved his hand to get the conductor's attention.

Claude Vidal swung around to see who dared to interrupt his set, but his annoyance turned to sheer delight when he laid eyes on Dora's svelte figure.

"Theodora!" he trilled in a heavy French accent. He rushed down the stairs and swept her into a hug. "Mon Dieu! You're the last person I expected to see here."

"Are you avoiding me on purpose?" Dora gasped, flattening her hand against her chest. "My dear friend Claude comes to my playground and doesn't bother to even drop a line to say salut! Have I done something to anger you?"

Claude bussed her cheeks three times in the French style and hugged her again. "You have made me furious! Abandoning Paris without even a by your leave! If anyone is to be offended, it is me."

By now, the trumpet player had joined the group. He edged Claude aside and took Dora's hands in his, swallowing her slender fingers in his dark-skinned grip. "I thought I saw a ghost when you walked up to the stage. But no, it is you. The gossip is true. Our favourite chanteuse relinquished her swinging ways to become a prim and proper English girl."

"Please tell me that's a lie," Fitz blurted, reminding the rest of them he was still there.

Dora slapped him on the wrist. "Of course, it's a horrible, vicious lie. I could no more change my ways than a leopard could lose its spots. The truth is, I was due for a change of scene. Now, enough gabbing. Strike up a tune and let these good people dance again. We can have a proper chat after their bedtime."

Dora let Fitz guide her across the dance floor during the first song. When he spotted his wife across the room, he handed her over to another of his friends. Round and round Dora went, each song finding her paired with a new partner. Some required a firm grip to trap their wandering hands. Others stuttered and sweated from being so close in proximity to the darling of London's social scene.

The fourth time a man trod on her toes, she acquiesced to his suggestion they avail themselves of a glass of punch and a breath of fresh air. There was no sign of Rex. Dora only hoped that he was having better luck at gathering information. There were plenty of men and women standing along the garden terrace, but having rushed outside without even a wrap, Dora felt goose-pimples rise on her arms.

She considered and just as quickly dismissed any thought of sticking it out. With her teeth chattering from the frosty evening air, she was unlikely to be a delightful conversationalist. When she spied her brother Benedict across the way, that sealed the decision. His emerald eyes widened in shock and he gave every sign of preparing to march her way.

Dora slid through the nearest door and slithered through the crowd. But in her haste to distance herself from her bossy older brother, she swept past the band. Claude got a glimpse of her strawberry blonde bob and waved for her to join him on stage.

She knew what he intended. With a deft hand, he guided the tune to a close and quieted the crowd so he might address the room.

"Lords, Ladies, and Gentlemen, tonight you are in for a rare treat. Ma chère amie and chanteuse extraordinaire, Mademoiselle Theodora Laurent, has agreed to grace us with a single song. What will it be?" He looked at Dora and waited with bated breath.

Dora played her role to a tee, replying with the line she'd used many times before. "What else but Mon Homme? I might even go so far as to dedicate it to my special someone."

Claude clapped his hands in satisfaction with her choice. Once again, he addressed the room. "Fanny Brice took the world by storm last year with the English translation. But as a true Frenchman, I must say it pales in comparison to the original."

By then, the orchestra members had shifted their chairs to clear a space for Dora at the front of the stage. Claude lifted his baton to tick off the rhythm. The brass and drums faded into the background when Dora's husky voice lilted through the air.

Dora sang the lines from memory, her French flawless as she waxed poetic about her man. Between the music and the song, Dora closed her eyes and imagined herself back in Paris, sipping wine and singing songs until the wee hours of dawn.

But much like those adventures, so too did the song reach its end. She held the last note until it alone lingered in the air. No sooner did she close her mouth and open her eyes did the dancers break into a round of applause.

She bowed as expected, all the while scanning the faces at the back of the room, wondering whether Rex had witnessed her performance. But in the end, it wasn't his piercing blue eyes and aquiline nose that caught her attention.

That honour went to a middle-aged woman wearing a drop-waist, navy satin gown and sapphires around her neck. The bold colours only emphasised the paleness of her skin. Her mouth was half open, her body frozen in shock.

Dora knew exactly how she felt. Because that woman, known to all the world as the Adaline Cavendish, Duchess of Dorset, also answered to another name.

Mama.

Chapter 9
The hasty escape

Meanwhile, on the other end of the house...

The crowd thinned as soon as Rex exited the main entrance and made his way into the west wing of the home. It wasn't so much that there were fewer people in general as there was a complete absence of women, particularly once he passed the door to the library and sitting room. The game room and FitzClarence's study had been unofficially declared the domain of the men.

Boisterous tones echoed from inside the game room, so that was where Rex went first. Rex wasn't typically the type to note the decor, but the juxtaposition of hunting game and parlour games caught him off guard. A stuffed lion's head held place of honour above the crackling fireplace. Around the room, the walls were decorated with more hunting trophies, mounted weapons, and an impressive Rubens hunting scene that dominated one wall. Yet the furniture included a snooker table, a dartboard, and plenty of comfortable seating.

The dozen or so men in the room looked as though they were facing off for battle, but Rex soon realised it was a war of words and not of shots. Half the men stood on the right side of the room, leaning against the billiard table. The other half occupied a seating area furnished with leather sofas.

In the middle of the room, two men stood nearly nose to nose, arguing vociferously with one another.

Rex paused in the entry, unsure where he should stand. While skimming the room, a flutter of motion caught his attention. The Duke of Dorset, whom Rex recognised from the luncheon, waved for Rex to join him on the far side of the room.

Rex skirted around the crowd, pausing to pour himself a scotch from the cut glass decanter, and then scooted into place beside the towering duke, on the edge of the group near the fireplace. Standing this close to him, Rex couldn't help but think that the duke reminded him of someone. There was something about the shape of his patrician nose and his sly green eyes that scratched at the back of his mind.

The duke whispered, "I'm surprised to see a young whippersnapper like yourself in here. I'd expect you to be like my son Benedict, preferring to twirl women around the ballroom instead of engaging in pointless political debates."

Of course! The duke's son was Benedict Cavendish, whom Rex had met during his investigation of his friend's death earlier in the year.

"I may yet answer the siren's call of the music, but first I wanted to take advantage of the opportunity to further my political understanding."

The duke chuckled and shook his head. "The only thing you're likely to gain is a headache from listening to those two blowhards, but far be it from me to discourage the youth."

The men in the stand-off were none other than the Lord Godfrey and Lord Sutherland. Once again, the pair had locked horns over the question of the Soviets. Rex was cast back to his uni days, watching the members of the Oxford Union engage in their fierce debates.

The men hadn't changed their respective positions on the topic. Lord Sutherland roused the watchers with jeers about Lloyd George's intelligence, given his credence of the Soviet rumour. Lord Godfrey didn't so much defend the Prime Minister as argue that the situation in Russia was evolving, and they'd be fools to dismiss the country as a potential threat.

Rex hung on their every word. The longer the debate went on, the more he came to believe that the conservatives might be the brains behind the rumour. At least half of them seemed to give the Soviet risk a minimum of credence. His money was on Lord Godfrey, or one of the other men riding his proverbial coattails. He leaned first to one side, then the other, making note of the men standing on the other side of the room. Those he recognised, he committed to memory. For the rest, he marked their appearance in his mind by making note of any defining physical features.

His shifting stance didn't go unnoticed. The duke set his drink on a nearby table and, as soon as the debaters paused to draw breath, he clapped to get their attention. "Excellent points, old chaps. While I enjoy a hearty debate as much as the next man, it would serve us well to remember we are currently standing in the home of Lord FitzClarence and not in the halls of Westminster. I suggest, for the sake of our wives and daughters we've left abandoned on the dance floor, we draw this portion of the evening to a close."

His words garnered laughter around the room, and the crowd of men dispersed. Rex hung back and took advantage of the cover of conversation to ask the duke a question. "Do Sutherland and Godfrey often engage in these types of discussions?"

"Far too often for my tastes. Each would like to claim superiority over the other, while the rest of us all agree that the party is safest with them balanced. That is why we insisted on a hard and fast rule a few years back. The men are only allowed to publicly debate matters on which they can first find a common ground."

Rex did not know what that meant. "It didn't seem they had anything in common, at least, not based on what I heard today."

The duke waved him off. "That's only because you weren't there the day we learned about the intelligence regarding the Turks and Soviets. Within twenty-four hours, both arrived at the opinion that the intelligence was false. They agreed that no such threat should affect the British stance on the Chanak matter. Their opinions differed around the longer term possibilities for an antagonistic relationship with Russia."

Rex goggled. "Really? I thought for sure that Lord Godfrey took the threat seriously."

"No, he did not. If you want to find a man who found that nonsense to be of relevance to current affairs, I suggest you wander to Fitz's study where the Liberals have no doubt set up their own camp. Now, if you'll excuse me, I promised my wife a dance."

The duke's words reminded Rex how long he'd left Dora on her own, but he staved off any thoughts of tracking her down. Tonight might be his only chance to speak with Lloyd George's fellow party members in a relaxed environment. If the Duke of Dorset was correct, he'd have to search within the Prime Minister's party to understand why the rumour surfaced at all.

Could the Prime Minister himself be the one who made St Cecil spread the rumour? How badly had the man wanted to go to war? Was he desperate enough to make a fellow party member lie to give him an excuse?

Rex followed a trio of men out the door of the game room. When they turned toward the main part of the house, Rex headed in the other direction. The study was on the opposite side of the corridor, only a few steps down.

Rex only made it as far as the doorway before reality set in. What was he doing? He could hardly bluster his way into the middle of the half-dozen men smoking cigars and chatting in a low tone. While he recognised a few of the men, he wasn't acquainted with any of them well enough to sustain a sudden show of camaraderie.

Even if he did invite himself into the midst of the group, there was no guarantee they'd want to discuss politics. Unlike the conservative lords, these men were relaxed. Their expressions showed no great cares, and their tones no hint of disagreement.

He spun around to leave before anyone caught him lingering at the threshold and immediately spotted Dora hustling down the corridor. She had a bright smile pasted on her face, but it didn't match the wildness in her eyes. On anyone else, he'd have thought them panicked. But this was Dora. The woman was far too prepared for any and all outcomes. He was quite sure that panic wasn't part of her emotional repertoire.

"Darling! There you are!" Dora latched her hand onto his arm and practically dragged him into the study.

The sudden appearance of a female in their midst threw the men off-balance. Two men choked mid-drink while another almost swallowed his cigar.

Dora didn't let that stop her. She twiddled her fingers at the men and cooed, "Pardon us for bursting in, but Rexy-poo promised me a dance and the corridor is absolutely heaving with people." She glanced back at Rex and added, "Come along, darling man. We can cut across the terrace and make it in time for the tango."

It took all of Rex's coordination to keep up with Dora's speedy pace through the study. Dora had lied. Why? There'd hardly been anyone in the corridor, and there was certainly no need for them to rush. His questions, however, had to wait until they were out of earshot.

Dora all but flung open the door to the rear terrace. She kept going, leading him down the garden path, both literally and figuratively, until the boxed hedge of Fitz's English garden hid them completely from sight. Only then did she slow down enough to catch her breath.

"Is someone dead?" Rex blurted.

"No, but if we don't make tracks, I might end up that way."

"What?" Rex yelped. He choked back the rest of his question when Dora shushed him.

"I spotted someone capable of blowing my cover. I'll explain, but not now. We've got to get out of here, ideally without crossing paths with anyone else."

Rex had plenty of questions left, but Dora's fiery expression told him now wasn't the time. Instead of worrying about the who, what, and why, he turned his mind toward the how. "Follow me," he instructed. He led her deeper into the garden, pulling on his memories of past visits. He was fairly certain there was a side gate further ahead that opened onto the street.

Dora encouraged him to move faster, her teeth chattering in the chilly evening air. "Do you know where the car is?"

"Haven't a clue, but if you can lower yourself to riding in a hire car, I'll flag a taxi for us."

"I've ridden in far worse than that, but Rex, you can't come."

Rex was so intent on finding the gate that he didn't process her words until he'd located the item in question. The door was barred and locked, but Rex didn't let that slow him. He remembered the time Fitz revealed he kept a key hidden under a rock. While he searched the hard, cold ground in the pitch dark shadow, he asked her what she meant by her remark.

"Our coats are still inside. If we leave them behind, we might as well wave a flag and announce we sneaked out. And even if that weren't the case, there is still another matter to take into consideration."

Rex gave a cry of satisfaction when he located the smooth stone with the key attached underneath. He hoisted it into the air, earning a sigh of relief from Dora. He turned to put the key into the gate, but stopped to clarify one thing. "Not leaving behind our coats, I understand. But for the life of me, I can't come up with a second reason for me to go back."

Dora unwrapped her arms from where she was hugging herself against the cold long enough to prop her hands on her hips and glare at Rex. "Besides being my favourite, that coat is a priceless Siberian sable gifted to me by an exiled Russian Grand Duke. I can hardly pop over to Regent Street and pick up a replacement."

Rex knew better, but he couldn't stop himself from asking, "Why did an exiled Romanov gift you a fur coat?"

Dora sidled up against him, snuggling into his warmth. He tilted his head down so he could look her full in the face. She was so close that he could feel her breath on his cheeks.

"Someday, if you are very, very lucky, I will show you. But for now, I'll leave you with this. The Grand Duke adored exploring the contrast between my silky ivory skin and the soft ebony fur."

Rex was utterly helpless against the mental image of Dora dressed only in furs. He didn't notice she'd slipped out the gate until she whistled for a taxi and then shouted that she'd see him tomorrow.

While the woman herself disappeared into the confines of a black cab, Rex knew that wouldn't be the last time he saw her that night. Thanks to her parting words, he fully expected her to play a starring role in his dreams.

Chapter 10
A night at Club 43

Dora was much more herself by mid-afternoon of the following day. She'd gone to sleep, fully expecting to receive a terse note from her mother when she awoke. Even worse, she half feared her mother would turn up in person and demand a lengthy explanation.

Yet, her concerns were for naught, as neither her mother nor any notes appeared. There were two potential explanations. The first was that she'd been mistaken and her mother's emotions had everything to do with the words of the song instead of the woman singing them. The second, admittedly more likely scenario, had Dora's brother Benedict physically restraining their mother from bursting in.

The mental image that idea evoked was enough to bring a smile to Dora's face, thereby smoothing the last of the worry lines from her forehead.

Rex turned up shortly after, looking very dapper in a navy suit, grey waistcoat, and red and navy striped tie. The dark colour of his suit made the blue of his eyes that much more noteworthy.

"I'm much relieved you made it home safely," he said after

he joined Dora in her library. "And before you ask, I left your fur with Harris on my way in."

"Aren't you a darling?" Dora patted the cushion beside her on the sofa. "You needn't worry overmuch about me. Whenever I go out, I make a point to tuck a switchblade in my stockings."

"I... don't know what to say in response, except that I hope you've never had cause to use it."

"Of course not! Don't be silly," Dora said. If believing that helped Rex sleep better, who was she to stain his thoughts with the ugly truth? "Inga and Harris will be here momentarily, so save any discoveries until they join us. Did you at least have an enjoyable evening, my mad dash from the event aside?"

"Unexpectedly, I did. It's been ages since I went to a high society shindig. Now that everyone sees me as entangled with you, I don't have to worry about any of the mothers setting me in their sights. I was able to catch up with old school chums, speak with more of the politicos, and make the most of Fitz's excellent stock of brandy. The only negative was I never got that dance with you."

"We'll have plenty of opportunities to sway cheek-to-cheek in the future." Given Dora was a keen to take a spin in Rex's arms, she'd make sure of it.

The sound of the tea trolley trundling along the wooden floors put paid to any further discussions. In short order, Harris and Inga were settled comfortably on a sofa of their own and everyone had a fresh cup of tea in hand.

"Rex, you're up first. Were you able to make any progress last night in our search for Murdoch's killer?"

"I learned a few things. It seems fortune smiled on me, ensuring I was in the right place at the right time."

"On more than one occasion," Dora added, interrupting him. "But let's keep our focus on the business at hand. Tell us what you learned."

Rex needed no further prompting to recount the debate between Lords Sutherland and Godfrey. While he spoke, Dora only half listened. The rest of her was too busy thanking the stars that Rex hadn't asked why she'd left so abruptly.

After their months together, with the pair working side-by-side and Rex always rising to the task, he'd more than proven his trustworthiness. If she told him her real identity, he wouldn't blab it to the world. But that didn't make her any more eager to come clean about who she was — Dorothy Cavendish, daughter of the Duke of Dorset and widow of the Viscount Lisle.

Rex was enamoured of Theodora Laurent. He hung on her words and his eyes watched her wander about a room. If she returned to plain old Dorothy, would his interest flag? She'd find out someday, but the longer she put off that eventuality, the better.

Now, however, she needed to pay attention to what he was saying. Fortunately, she tuned in right as he arrived at the crux of the story, when an all-too-familiar name caught her ear.

"The Duke of Dorset was kind enough to share a critical piece of information. Despite their vociferous arguments over the future risk of the Russian threat, neither Godfrey nor Sutherland gave credence overlong to the rumour of the Soviet involvement with the Turks. He suggested I speak with the men in Lloyd George's party. That's where I was going when you found me."

"Were you able to speak with them later?" Dora asked, feeling somewhat guilty for her part in distracting Rex from his duty.

"No. They'd dispersed to other areas of the house by the time I made my way back. However, that isn't necessarily a bad thing. I was coming up short of a way to introduce the topic, given I barely knew their names."

"I'm sure we can think up something if we put our heads

together." Dora shifted her gaze to Inga. "Any suggestions of where to start?"

"The leading Liberal peers are James Newberry and Simon St Cecil. It's too soon for Rex to approach St Cecil directly, but Newberry isn't a bad idea."

"Newberry, you say..." Dora tapped her index finger against her lips. "Stay put for a moment while I go check something."

Dora triggered the release to open the hidden door into her private study. There, she rifled through a stack of mail until she found a card she'd received a week earlier. With it in hand, she next searched through her desk drawer until she pulled free a paper covered in dense text. She compared the notes on the paper against the date on the invite and nearly squealed in delight. She did so love it when a plan came together.

Back again in the library, she held the card against her chest, preventing Rex from seeing the wording embossed on the front. "What would you say if I knew not only where we can find Lord Newberry this evening, but I can also guarantee we can have a conversation with him?"

"I'd say I'd be impressed, but based on the way you're hiding that invite from me, something tells me you've left off some of the details."

"That's because we'll need a little help. Luckily for us both, Harris here is more than qualified. Right?" Dora circled the sofa, coming around to hand Harris the card.

Harris skimmed the text and then burst out laughing. "Brilliant, Dora! I presume you checked the staff rota?"

"Indeed. She'll be there. Therefore, he'll be there. Now all we need is an appropriate wardrobe. What do you think? Ancient Greece? Brothers Grimm?"

"Hold on, now. Just hold on there," Rex interjected, rising to his feet. He marched over and plucked the card from Harris's hand. "Wait, a minute. This says Fancy Dress Dance. As much as I'd adore seeing you in a toga, I'd like an explanation first."

Dora returned to her spot and encouraged Rex to sit. She twisted to face him. "What's the first rule of spying?"

"Err, don't get caught?"

"Surprisingly, no. Perhaps it will help if I remind you it is a quote from Sir Francis Bacon." Dora waited for Rex to fill the gap, but her hint wasn't sufficient. "Knowledge itself is power, Rex. If you know which skeletons hide in the closets and where the bodies are buried, you can get yourself out of most any tight spot."

Rex raised his eyebrows and gave her a nod of admiration. "Point well made. Enlighten me, please. What knowledge are you using right now?"

"I'm chummy with Kate Meyrick of Club 43, but I failed to mention I'm also an investor in her business. In return for a steady stream of funds, I get information on the club regulars and their latest entanglements. Lord Newberry happens to be enraptured by one of Kate's dancing girls — Penelope is her stage name. Penelope's on the rota for this evening. I'd be shocked if Lord Newberry wasn't in attendance, as well."

Rex smiled, but almost as quickly his expression soured. "Oh no. I've realised the implications of what you're saying. We have to go in costume, don't we? Please, don't make me an ancient deity!"

"Deity?" Harris replied. "With a nickname like Rex? I had something more regal in mind. Dora, do you still have that heavy kohl eyeliner and the scarab pin?"

"Aren't you brilliant! Absolutely, I do, although it might take me some time to unearth it. I haven't seen it since we moved in here. Inga, you'll be a doll and help me hunt through the unopened boxes, right?"

Dora didn't need to ask twice. Rex was still doing his guppy impersonation when Dora delivered him into Harris's expert hands. It took the rest of the day for each pair to assemble the pieces of their respective assigned costume. After a pause for a hearty dinner of sausage, mash, gravy and steaming Yorkshire puddings, the two spies retired to separate bedrooms to don their clothes.

They split as Dora and Rex and met again as Cleopatra and Julius Caesar. Dora knew better than to tease him, but that didn't stop her from whistling at Rex's bare legs beneath his white Roman gown and metal breastplate.

For once, Rex didn't mind. He was too busy ogling Dora's curves, so elegantly displayed by the Egyptian dress. The sky-high slit up the skirt rendered the floor-brushing length moot.

Harris and Inga stood arm in arm, admiring the young couple. They were as proud as if they'd been their parents. Harris moved away long enough to tighten the straps on the breastplate. "I don't want to jinx things by speaking out of term, but Inga, even you have to admit they've got a shot at winning the grand prize."

"I'll be utterly despondent if they don't," Inga replied, smiling at her beau. "Now get out of here before Rex's good sense kicks in and he demands a change of clothes."

Harris hustled them out the door and into the waiting Mercedes roadster Dora had recently bought. They barely had time to get comfortable in the car's leather seats before Harris stopped on Gerard Street at the innocuous door numbered forty-three.

Dora turned her nose up at the line of people waiting to get inside and sauntered past them. The hulking man with the crooked nose guarding the entrance had the door open for her before she uttered a word.

"Evening, Miss Laurent. Mrs Meyrick said to tell you she

has your preferred table reserved and your guest already seated."

"Thank you, Tommy. Please give my regards to that adorable wife of yours. Has she had the little one yet?"

"No, ma'am, but it'll be any day now."

Dora wasn't done. "You make sure Kate sends me a note when congratulations are in order. Auntie Theodora will send a little gift."

Rex kept quiet until they'd surrendered their coats and hat at the coat check. "How did you know about his..."

"Wife?" Dora finished his sentence. She reached up and patted him on the cheek. "I told you, Rexy. Knowledge is power. All knowledge, not only the bits that seem important."

Dora and Rex descended straight to the basement, where the band was in full swing. Between the low lights and the costumed figures, Dora gave thanks she'd had the foresight to ask the club proprietress to seat Lord Newberry at her regular table.

Located in one of the two alcoves, it was a long walk to the bar, but had the advantage of being supremely private. Rex slipped the server a pound note and the matter of drinks was settled.

"Is that one of the men you saw last night?" Dora asked, practically shouting into Rex's ear so he'd hear her.

"Yes, I recognise him."

"Excellent. We won't have long before his paramour finishes her set. Follow my lead." Dora swung her hips, giving hints of smooth flesh with every step, and ignored everyone except the man at her table.

Given he was seated, Dora couldn't accurately judge his height. But his thick head of white hair and flushed cheeks spoke of a life well-lived. He wore a hooded cloak and had a wand resting beside his glass. His eyes lit up when Dora stepped into his line of sight.

"Lord Newberry," Dora trilled in a breathy French accent. "Or should I say Merlin? What a delight! Kate always finds the most fascinating people to share my table, but she's outdone herself with you!"

"Miss Laurent, Lord Reginald," Newberry bobbed his head in greeting. He scooted over in the booth, making space for the pair of them to sit. "Dressing as Cleopatra and Marc Antony? Are you making a statement about ill-fated romance?"

Dora twisted around to glare at Rex in exasperation. "I told you that you should have worn the laurel wreath crown. How else will people know you're Caesar and not his second in command?"

"The crown itched, dear. And before you offer an alternate suggestion, no, I am not open to spilling wine on my tunic to fake stab wounds."

Lord Newberry laughed riotously at their banter, guffawing loud enough that the nearest dancing couple stopped to look their way. "I'd heard you two were droll, but you've exceeded your reputations. I'm surprised you'd make time for an old man such as myself. I'm hardly part of your normal set."

Dora swatted Newberry's arm. "If rumours about you and Penelope are correct, you're younger at heart than we are. Besides that, you're one of the few people here who is a still a relative stranger to me. Since you are dressed as Merlin, perhaps you'd be willing to entertain us with stories of secret meetings among the Knights of the Round Table."

"More like old men at the table," Newberry replied. "Lord Reginald, was it you I spotted in the Peers' Dining Hall this week?"

"Yes, it was. I find myself with a burgeoning interest in

political affairs, and a day in the Lords did little to whet my appetite."

"Despite the best efforts of the Tories," Dora added. "Can you imagine any man of mine affiliating with a party that calls itself conservative?"

"I couldn't agree more. Lord Reginald, you must give me a chance to make the case for the Liberal way of thinking. I'll tell you what. Why don't you join me for a drink tomorrow evening at my club? That is, if you don't have plans with this ravishing creature."

"He does, but I suppose I can give him a night off every once in a while. Now, enough of this boring work talk. I've got a bottle of champers with my name on it behind the bar. Rex, you can spin me around the floor while we work up a thirst."

Rex tossed his hands up and declared himself game. "It's a hard lot keeping up with her, but someone has to do it."

Lord Newberry shook his head in amazement. "I wouldn't complain too loudly, my boy. I may be too old for Miss Laurent now, but I know the type well. She may purr like a kitten, but step out of line and you'll find her claws are razor sharp."

Dora leaned over the table, giving Lord Newberry a flash of her cleavage. She addressed her remarks to him, but said them loud enough for Rex to hear.

"As much as I appreciate being compared to a lioness, I should warn you of one thing. Cats have a mind of their own, and they can never, ever be leashed."

Chapter 11
Dining with a peer

After a refreshing walk to stretch his legs and clear his mind, Lord Rex exited St James Square and stood across the street from The Reform Club. The traffic on Pall Mall was as busy as ever, but Rex plucked up his courage and hurried across during a rare break in the flow of vehicles. He was due to dine with Lord Newberry exactly on the hour, and he didn't want to be late.

The Reform Club was not a place Rex had visited before, despite having imagined himself there many a time as a young boy. Jules Verne had appropriated the club venue to use as the start and end point for Phileas Fogg's journey in *Around the World in Eighty Days*. In his younger years, Rex had imagined himself undertaking a similar heroic deed. While he certainly hoped that his search for Murdoch's killer wouldn't take him anywhere near that long, the idea that he might finish it here had a distinct appeal.

He hurried up the front steps to the front door of the imposing Palazzo-style building. The club's butler stood waiting in the antechamber. After confirming Rex's name was on the guest list, he showed him to the so-called coffee room where Lord Newberry was waiting for him to join.

The dining room's decor stood in stark contrast to the simple name. Red carpet decorated with gold braid flowed across the floor. Ionic columns limned in gold soared up the walls until they brushed the crown-moulding of the ceilings. The curtains of the windows were still open, allowing glimpses of the discreet gardens where members enjoyed a breath of fresh air.

Lord Newberry was seated at a table for two in the middle of the room. They'd spaced the tables far enough apart to allow the diners to converse without risk of being overheard. This was, indeed, one of the benefits of belonging to such a prestigious institution.

"Lord Reginald, I'm so pleased you made it. I worried you might regret accepting my invitation after dancing the night away with Miss Laurent."

"Please, call me Rex. As for regrets, I'm far from it. All things in balance, I say. And besides, there is only so much time with Theodora that one man can survive. She is most certainly a force."

"That's for sure. Without disparaging your most excellent costumes, I must admit that your win of grand prize in the fancy dress contest had as much to do with Miss Laurent's flash of skin and seductive smile. I'd say that if I were a few years younger, I'd give you a run for your money. However, not even in my twenties would I have been capable of handling such a woman."

"You seemed happy enough with Penelope, was it?"

"Oh yes, she's a doll. But enough about last night. Shall we order? I recommend starting with the Coquilles Saint-Jacques, before enjoying the club's infamous Lamb Cutlets Reform with sides of Heritage carrots and triple-cooked chips."

"That suits me fine. I'll let you order for us both."

After ordering their dinners and sitting comfortably while the waiter poured them glasses of their selected wine, Lord Newberry asked Rex why he had this sudden interest in politics.

Rex debated telling him the same tale he had told everyone else. It had the advantage of immediately shifting the conversation onto the desired topic. However, on his walk over, he'd given the matter much thought. He'd remembered one of Dora's favourite methods for inviting people to confide in her. As he looked across the table into Lord Newberry's open expression, and decided to take the risk.

"If I'm being honest, my interest dates back to my days at the war front. My rank allowed me the rare opportunity to be in the room when decisions were made about what tactics to use, whom to trust, and the importance of knowing when to act versus when to wait. When the war ended and I came home, I found myself once again living my normal, relatively aimless daily life. I was nearly on the brink of abandoning all hope of ever finding anything that could equally capture my interest, but then Theodora suggested I try my hand at politics."

"Miss Laurent has an interest in politics?" Lord Newberry shook his head in disbelief.

"Her only interest is in rubbing shoulders with them," Rex replied with a laugh. "But one only has to look to the society pages to realise just how many consequential figures she has met over the years. After I prattled on for long enough, she said if I was so interested in the country's direction, why not go into politics? I broached the idea with my grandmother and she wholeheartedly endorsed it. As you can imagine, those two don't agree very often, so I took that as a sign. I reached out within my circle of acquaintance to see if anyone was available to provide me with an introduction."

"The Dowager Duchess and London's favourite femme fatale agreed on something, and the world is still turning?"

Lord Newberry was so caught off guard that Rex didn't have the heart to tell him that the women had not only met, but actually got along like two peas in a pod. The well-timed arrival of the server with their dishes provided Rex time to gather his thoughts.

After the men scraped the last of the scallops baked in white wine and Gruyere from the decorative shells, the conversation returned to the previous matter.

"You'll forgive me if I can't let this go," Lord Newberry said by way of beginning. "Knowing your grandmother and Miss Laurent as well as I do, I'm shocked they were fine with you starting your discussions with the Conservative party."

"That was more of a happy accident than the result of any grand design. If you must know the truth, the blame lies entirely with Lord Audley. Audley was my commander while stationed at Le Touquet. His lordship is very highly regarded, so I took a risk and sent him a note. I still can't believe he agreed to introduce me around. It was on my first visit to the House of Lords with Lord Audley that we ran into Lord Godfrey. If we'd bumped into you in the corridor, the situation would have been entirely different."

"I am much relieved to hear you don't owe any allegiance to the Conservative party. I'll do my best tonight to convince you to give the Liberals a fair chance."

"I haven't closed my mind to any possible outcome," Rex assured Lord Newberry. He held back while the waiter swapped their empty plates for the entrée. After a few bites of the lamb, Rex spoke again. "I have to admit to being somewhat concerned by the recent events in Turkey. Granted, I am still very new to all the discussions about foreign affairs. But I was witness to a vociferous debate between Lords Sutherland and

Godfrey at the recent soirée. The men were highly critical of the Prime Minister and his advisers for their willingness to give credence to the rumour about the Soviets."

Lord Newberry leaned forward and pitched his voice low. "I will tell you I was similarly concerned when I heard about it initially. So much so that I went to visit my colleague St Cecil to see what he was about. St Cecil didn't appreciate me questioning him, that's for sure. He assured me that the source of the rumour was impeccable. As much as the Conservatives enjoy casting aspersions on Lloyd George, if anything, their ongoing debates only further underscore that the Soviets are not to be dismissed."

Before Rex got out a word, Lord Newberry raised his hand to flag down the waiter. While the pair debated which vintage of wine to try next, Rex watched his opportunity to get the answer to his all-important question evaporate before his eyes.

No sooner did Lord Newberry settle on a wine than he tossed out a query of his own. "How well do you know Lord Audley?"

Rex had thought himself prepared for any turn in the discussion, but this was a question he hadn't foreseen. He stumbled through as best as he could. "Does anyone know Audley well? I attended several evenings of debate while stationed in Le Touquet, but that is as far as any personal connection goes. Lord Audley isn't exactly known for being effusive with his gestures of friendship."

Lord Newberry chuckled and agreed that Rex made a good point. "I wish I had more opportunities to speak with him in depth, but my decision to join the Liberal party effectively curtailed any hope of having a close friendship. Everyone knows that Lord Audley is a defiant cross-bencher."

"Please don't hate me, but Lord Audley's non-conformist position is what interests me most about the man. I can see the benefits of remaining free of any entanglements which might otherwise force me to support a stance or an issue with which I don't agree."

"Yes, that is certainly a risk. However, as one of these senior advisers to my party, I have a voice in the party's decisions. While this in no way ensures I will always get my way, it does work out more times than not. I bet if I looked back into the numbers, I'd find myself in agreement with the Prime Minister's position on matters upwards of 90% of the time."

"How do you handle the remaining 10%?"

"There are times when I have to hold my nose and fall in line with the party's decisions. In a few very rare cases, I had to go so far as to do things that I found downright unpalatable. What carries me through is knowing that everything I do is for the greater good, not only for my party but for all of England. Although I'm sure he'd ruffle his feather, but in many ways, I am no different from Lord Audley. We simply disagree on the best way to serve the country." Lord Newberry wiped the last vestiges of gravy from his mouth and motioned again for the waiter.

"Would you care to peruse the dessert menu this evening, your grace?" the server asked.

Rex declined when Lord Newberry glanced his way. Lord Newberry followed suit, and with that, their dinner was at an end. Or so Rex thought. Instead, Newberry put forth a proposal.

"Would you care to join me in the club library for a glass of port and a cigar? Or do you need to rush off?"

"I've nowhere to be this evening other than here."
Especially until Rex discovered the source of the false rumour.

Along the way to the library, Rex passed several men whom he recognised from the House of Lords. He made note of their affiliation with the party in case he failed to get the name he sought that evening.

Little did Rex imagine that when he arrived in the library, he'd find the Prime Minister and Winston Churchill already there.

Dora would relish an opportunity to question such a powerful man, but Rex wasn't Dora. Finding himself in close confines with the Prime Minister and two of his most senior advisers took a heavy toll on Rex's confidence. It also put paid to any remaining aspirations of learning the truth.

There was no way he could come right out and ask these men why they'd been so willing to believe the false information. He didn't dare even mention St Cecil's name. Instead of getting the answer to his question, he wound up listening to Lloyd George rail for more than an hour about the difficulties of guiding the current coalition government. He claimed the Conservatives were actively plotting against him, but offered no proof when asked.

When a footman interrupted Lloyd George to deliver a message, Rex took the opportunity to make his goodbyes. His head was full of information, but he feared that none of it was useful to his current challenge. Despite having come so close to the Prime Minister and his leading advisors, he left with empty hands. Why hadn't St Cecil been there?

On his way back to his car, Rex consoled himself by remembering that he had Dora. He decided to go by her house that evening and tell her everything that he'd learned. Given Dora's knowledge of affairs, both local and foreign, she might be capable of unearthing a nugget of information that he'd overlooked.

If all else failed, at least her smiling face would leave him with a happier end to his evening.

Chapter 12
Lord Audley goes for a walk

Dora lit the wick of the gas lamp and turned the fire down to the lowest setting, casting the room in an amber glow. She invited Rex to join her on the comfortable sofa in her hidden study.

Alone, in the near dark, Rex sat as far from her as possible, clearly not trusting himself with her current state of undress.

Dora stifled a giggle and tucked her feet underneath her. She had never considered the black silk pyjamas cut in a masculine style she was currently wearing to be particularly feminine. But if the cross-eyed expression on Rex's face when she came down the stairs was any sign, the pyjamas were much more flattering than she thought.

"How was your dinner with Lord Newberry?"

Rex's recap was far too short for her liking. She trawled through his memories, asking question after question, but still came up dry. The only interesting bit was Lloyd George's complaints about his cabinet.

As for the rest, there was little there that was new.

Dora grabbed a notepad and pen. "Unless you disagree, I

say we strike Lord Newberry from our list of likely sources. If he'd passed the information along to St Cecil, he certainly wouldn't have mentioned going to see him for more details. It is interesting that he told you St Cecil got huffy. However, there's a world of distance between a getting your back up and being concerned enough to kill someone. That puts us right back at the Conservative peers. They are certainly making the most of the rumour being false."

Rex let out a breath. "Yes, but why would St Cecil keep quiet if either Sutherland or Godfrey were his source? Wouldn't he call them out for peddling the lie to him in the first place? As far as I can see, those two are far more interested in arguing with one another than giving credence to the rumour. The only one I'm unsure about is the Duke of Dorset."

"Don't waste your time," Dora replied. When Rex raised his eyebrows, she explained, "Dorset is Audley's arch-nemesis. He was likely the first person Audley investigated."

"That leaves us with St Cecil, where we still have no clue what he gains from the matter. What do you suggest we do next? I suppose I could try to speak to him, assuming I can arrange to bump into him at the House of Lords."

Dora shrugged her shoulders. It wasn't the worst plan she'd ever heard, but that didn't mean that it was any good. If nothing else, it risked putting Rex in the line of fire. "Before we go any further, we should reach out to Lord Audley. You never know, he may have some tidbit of information we can use to coax Lord Newberry into telling us more."

"In that case, I should let you get some rest. Will you send me a message when you've heard from Lord Audley?"

"I'll do you one better." Dora glanced at the clock on the wall and noted the time. "If we hurry, we should be able to catch his grace on his way home from his mistress's house. When the weather is clear, he prefers to walk. It will be easy as pie to pull up beside him and offer him a ride."

When Dora stood to leave, Rex pulled a face. "If I might make a suggestion, why don't you take a moment to change into something warmer while I go start the motor?"

Although it would have been entertaining to insist she go as she was, Dora opted to leave Rex in peace. "Brill! I'll be out in two blinks an eye."

Back upstairs in her room, Dora made quick work of swapping her pyjama bottoms for a pair of custom tailored men's trousers. In the interest of time, she pulled a wool jumper over her silk pyjama top. She topped the outfit off with the man's winter coat and considered the task accomplished. On her way to the stairs, she made a quick detour to Inga and Harris's room to alert them that she was heading out.

As agreed, Rex had the motor running. As soon as she closed her car door, he turned on his headlights and pulled out into the street.

"You'll have to tell me where to go," Rex said.

"Audley's mistress occupies a lavish flat on Bourdon Street in Mayfair. Are you familiar with the area?"

"Near Berkeley Square, right?" Rex circled around the Wellington Arch and angled the Rolls toward Mayfair. He navigated the streets of the posh neighbourhood until he located the correct one. At Dora's behest, Rex pulled up the car into an open space along the side of the pavement, a few doors shy of the correct number.

"Audley's car is not waiting out front. That's a good sign. Stop here for a moment while I go make sure he hasn't left yet."

Rex scrunched his face. "How will you figure that out? Are you going to knock on the door?"

"Of course not," Dora scoffed. She wagged a finger at him. "I'll be able to tell based on which windows are still lit up upstairs. I keep telling you, Rex. Every piece of information has value."

Dora grabbed a man's hat from the seat beside her and pulled it onto her head. She flipped up the collar of her coat, fully concealing her strawberry blonde hair. Only then did she exit the car. She hurried up the street, glanced up at the house in question, counting the windows, and then made haste to get back to Rex.

"We are in luck. He appears to be running longer this evening. You might as well turn off the engine so that we don't attract attention while we wait."

"How much longer do you think he might be?"

"Not sure. Perhaps another fifteen minutes, or at most, half an hour. He's always home before midnight. I don't recommend asking him whether his carriage turns into a pumpkin, however. He has little sense of humour when it comes to his love life."

Rex reared back with his eyes wide opened. "You actually had the temerity to say that?"

"Oh please, that's the least of what I've said to Lord Audley over the years. Believe it or not, I think he actually enjoys our banter. Who else in the British Empire would dare to poke fun at the great and laudable Lord Audley, Duke of Montagu? I'm practically duty-bound to remind him he is human. Goodness knows, no one else ever will."

"If it's all the same, I'll leave that task for you and you alone."

Dora chuckled at Rex's timidity. "Darling, I consider it one of life's pleasures. I'd no sooner surrender the task of keeping Audley humble to you than I'd swear off gin or pledge to give up dancing. Trust me, once you get over your fear of who he is, you'll find out he puts his trousers on one leg at a time, just like the rest of us."

As if to illustrate Dora's point, Lord Audley chose that

moment to emerge from his mistress's flat. From their viewpoint, Dora watched Audley skip down the front steps with the grace of a much younger man. Spending time with his companion always did him good. It was why Dora had taken such great care to memorise his habits.

Dora didn't notice the sound of the approaching car motor until the dark-coloured vehicle sped past. When it squealed to a stop directly in front of Lord Audley, Dora paid attention. Therefore, she had a front-row seat when two men leapt from the car, both dressed in black coats and hats. In the darkness, their features were little more than shadows.

"What in the??" Rex blurted. He reached for the starter button, but Dora staid his hand.

It would take far too long to get the motor running. Already, the men were dragging Lord Audley into their car.

Like Rex, Dora wanted to rush to Audley's aid, but her years of training held her locked in place. Those men might have guns. Right now, Dora's only advantage was that they didn't know she was there watching. If they took her out, who would be capable of finding Audley?

Within seconds, the car sped off into the night, turning right at the end of the street and disappearing into London's maze of streets.

Dora had a live wire of pure electricity running from her head to her toes. Despite all their precautions, Audley was gone, snatched off the street before her very own eyes. Still, she could hardly believe it. She desperately wanted to think it had been a training exercise designed to test her and Rex.

But playing games was not Audley's style. And the white handkerchief that had covered his face had been authentic enough. She'd seen him jerk his head back and then slump, helpless to save himself.

Her thoughts flickered through her mind in a maddening

carousel of images. These people had come prepared. They'd known exactly when, where, and how to capture one of England's most senior advisors. Even now, the street was again silent. No one called out a shout of alarm.

That was fine. There were sirens enough in Dora's head. She wrenched open her car door and leapt onto the sidewalk, urging Rex to follow suit. His years of military service served them well. He did as commanded without asking a single question.

Dora pushed her legs forward into a jog, a run, and then an all-out sprint. She forced herself to ease up long enough to huff out an explanation. "We have to get to Audley's. Secure it. Faster this way."

She was right. What would have been a leisurely ten-minute walk for Lord Audley, they covered in less than half the time. Dora tried the rear gate, but it was locked. No matter. A nearby brick wall offered enough toeholds for her and Rex to scale it with ease.

Dora knew every square foot of Audley's garden. She raced along the pathways until she spotted the stairwell leading down to the kitchen door. The room was dark, but four windows further along, she could see a light.

She knelt and rapped on the narrow window that provided sunlight to the rooms of the low floor.

A shadow moved inside the room. Dora darted back to the kitchen door, with Rex hot on her heels. A moment later. Walters, Audley's dignified butler, undid the latch and opened the door wide enough to make his displeasure with the late-night visit known.

"Audley's gone. Taken," Dora added, choking out the words between ragged breaths. Those were the magic words. The butler's face drained of colour. He stepped back, pulling the door open wider, and invited her in.

"The phone?" Dora asked.

"Help yourself."

Dora paused long enough to rattle off instructions for Rex to bar the rear door and then check the rest of the house. She knew where to find the phone. It was upstairs, in the front hall, near the entrance. Her footsteps echoed on the servant staircase, seeming loud enough to wake the dead. Still, the thump of her own heartbeat drowned out all else. She found the telephone and lifted the receiver. When the operator answered, she rattled off her own number and prayed someone would hear it ring.

An eternity passed. Inga's scratchy, sleep-ridden voice echoed over the line. "Hullo?"

Dora spoke the codewords they'd all committed to memory, but never expected to use. Somehow, her voice sounded perfectly normal.

"Inga, it's me. I've had an *odd evening*."

Inga's voice lost all traces of sleepiness. She'd understood the coded message. "We're on our way."

Dora replaced the handset and put the telephone back on the small table that had been set aside for its use. Her fingers, however, refused to obey her order for them to turn loose.

A flicker of panic-laced fear passed through her head. That alone was enough to shock her to her senses. She had many tasks to accomplish over the coming hours, but falling apart wasn't one of them. In and out, she filled her lungs and exhaled away the sour taste of worry. Her grip on the telephone loosened. Her back straightened, her shoulders squared, until she was once again her indomitable self.

Rex joined her in the corridor. His wild gaze calmed when he beheld her standing there, as carefree and in control as ever.

"What do we do now?" he whispered.

"We wait. Inga and Harris are on their way. As soon as they

get here, we'll put our heads together and figure out who has Lord Audley."

"And if we can't?"

Dora's steely gaze burned away the last vestiges of panic from Rex's mind.

"We can. We will. And God help whoever this is, because as soon as I find them, they're as good as dead."

Chapter 13
Dora gets serious

Dawn was fast approaching, but for Rex and Dora, sleep was still hours away. With the help of Inga, Harris, and Audley's servants, they had secured the house and posted guards. Thus far, there'd been no attempts at incursion. Dora wasn't sure whether that was a good thing or a bad one.

Rex's glum expression reflected the burning pain in the pit of his stomach. He could hardly bring himself to say the words. Yet, holding them back did little to erase them from his mind. Finally, he succumbed.

"Do you think he's... dead?"

Dora glanced up from the stack of papers she was perusing. "Dead? I should think not. If their intention was to end his life, they'd have done away with him there on the pavement. No, they took him for a reason. I wish I knew what it was."

Inga chose that moment to return to the library, bearing a tray of cups and saucers. The butler, Walters, followed behind with a steaming pot of coffee and a plate of pastries. From his stiff carriage, Rex surmised that the man was still uncomfortable with their presence. If it weren't for Audley's strict instructions about what to do in any cases of unexplained absence, the butler would have likely barred the door and left them outside.

Instead, Walters shifted side tables around until they all had a place to put their food and drink. With no further requests to accommodate, he let them get back to their work.

"Nothing here," Dora grumbled, closing the file she'd been searching. "I hate to admit it, but I'm flummoxed. Lord Audley has always been incredibly careful to keep the spy business at arm's length. Why would someone kidnap him? Why now?"

Rex stared into his coffee cup and half-wished it was tea instead. Perhaps the tea leaves would provide some clue. Under any other circumstances, he'd laugh in the face of such an outlandish suggestion. But now, he was willing to take all the help he could get.

He didn't need the others to say it. He was to blame. The guilt lay heavy across his shoulders. If anything, the longer they all went without saying a word, the worse he felt. Eventually, he gave in. "This is all my fault. I must have slipped up somewhere and given something away."

Dora dropped her stack of papers and rushed to his side. "No, Rex! How can you even think that?" She wrapped a silk-clad arm around his shoulders and squeezed tight.

Rex, however, was having none of it. He shrugged her off, twisting to look her in the eye. "How can I not? If I'd been more capable, Audley never would have had to accompany me to the House of Lords. No one would have known we were in any way connected. Instead, all everyone kept asking was how close is my connection with Lord Audley."

Inga waved a hand to halt him there. "What do you mean? I can understand Lord Godfrey wanting to know since Audley made the introductions between you two, but who else asked?"

"Lord Newberry."

Dora leaned forward. "Wait. You didn't mention this earlier. Tell me exactly what he said."

From the intense concentration on Dora's face, this had to be important. But he hadn't committed that part of their conversation to memory. The best he could do was share the highlights.

"Newberry asked how I ended up in the company of the Tories. I stuck to the truth. Audley accompanied me to Westminster. We ran into Lord Godfrey in the corridor. The rest was history. Newberry asked me a few questions about how well I knew Audley. I deflected them as best as I could and turned the conversation back to the topic of the Liberals. Dinner ended, we adjourned to the library, and you know the rest."

Dora and Inga exchanged inscrutable looks.

"What? What did I miss?" Rex asked.

"You may have provided the missing puzzle piece," Dora answered. "Newberry was far too interested in Lord Audley for my liking. It can't be a coincidence that only hours after your dinner together, Audley goes missing. Despite your efforts, Newberry must have surmised that Audley was behind your pointed questions. If he is working with St Cecil, it would explain why someone snatched Audley off the street. They had to prevent him from digging any further."

"But we crossed Newberry off the list!"

"That was before they kidnapped Audley. Now, everyone to whom you've spoken is going back on the list. I say we start with Newberry and go from there."

Dora's no-nonsense attitude soothed Rex's frazzled nerves.

"I'll do anything I can to help. Do you want me to invite him over or ask for another meeting? I'm sure he'd agree to my request."

"I'm sure he would, too," Dora replied. "However, this time

around, I don't want him to see us coming. That means we need to move fast. *Now fast.*"

Rex waited for her to explain what she meant, and she didn't leave him hanging. She leapt to her feet and began pacing around the room, while Rex and Inga looked on.

"I'd say we should come right out and ask Newberry if he's responsible, but there's no way he'll confess. Not unless we have unassailable proof that he was responsible for the false intelligence. But how can we get that?"

"You're making my head spin," Inga grumbled. "If you can stand still long enough, I might have a suggestion."

Dora stopped walking and turned to look at her best friend. She propped her hands on her hips. "Go on, I'm listening."

"I'll start with a question. What do you do when you need to lay a false trail regarding foreign intelligence?"

"Something that serious isn't a task I'd handle on my own. There'd be at least two of us. We'd need to prepare fake documents, doctor photographs, and plant rumours to support our case."

"Exactly!" Inga beamed. "And all those things leave a trail of their own. You need to stop asking and start searching. Check Newberry's private files and see what you can find."

Rex opened his mouth to say no, but Dora beat him to the punch. Except, instead of saying it was a crazy idea, she clapped her hands in delight.

"Oh, I do love undercover work. Be a doll and pass me the second folder down in the stack nearest you." Dora held out a hand until Inga offered the requested document. "Thanks to Audley's meticulous notes on the key individuals, we know exactly where Newberry's office is located. Let me find it..." Dora skimmed the page, with a smile creeping onto her face. "Hmm, do you want the good news or the bad first?"

Rex didn't need to think overlong before answering. "Good news, please. I need all of that I can get."

"It says here that the senior Liberals have a private meeting room. That gives us both Newberry and St Cecil — two birds with one stone."

That was most certainly excellent news. So much so that he was afraid to ask what she'd left off.

Inga spoke up. "It's best to rip off the bandage in one go. Tell him the bad news."

Dora pasted a wide smile on her face and did her best to generate some enthusiasm for what she said next. "The meeting room is in the Palace of Westminster. We're going there... Right now."

Rex reeled first one way and then the other. "Now? But it's only..." he checked his watch and added, "six in the morning. The offices won't open until nine." He looked first at Dora and then at Inga, waiting for one of them to see sense.

But instead of backing up, the pair exchanged one of their unreadable glances, conveying a multitude of words he didn't understand. Whatever was about to happen, he wasn't going to like.

"Excellent point. Time's a-ticking and we're sitting around here like old hens." Dora scooped the papers from the table and shoved them into a crate.

"I'll tell Harris to fetch the car," Inga added. "I suppose you'll need Cynthia's assistance. I'd better ring to make sure she's awake."

With every word, Rex grew more and more bewildered, until he stood it no longer. "What are you doing? No, wait. What are we doing?"

Dora glanced from the desk drawer she was rifling through. "I already told you. We're going to Westminster to search the Liberals' office. We've got a narrow window to get in and out without getting caught, but I have faith we can do it."

"But you're still wearing half of your pyjamas!"

"That's why Harris is bringing round the car. We'll speed to my house, change into our clerical staff disguises, have Cynthia falsify a permission slip for us, and then we'll be ready to infiltrate the palace. Westminster, that is. Not Buckingham. That would require an entirely different plan."

Rex spluttered, having no idea which of her statements to address first. In the end, he went with the one that bewildered him the most. "You have a plan for breaking into Buckingham Palace?"

Dora straightened up, put something into her pocket, and bumped the drawer closed with her hip. "Darling, I've got a plan for breaking in to most anywhere important. But those are nowhere near as interesting as my ideas for how to break out!"

She swept around the desk and latched her arm around Rex's waist, propelling him to the door. "Now we really must hurry. As I said, this plan will go so much more smoothly if we can search the files without a half dozen staffers looking on."

Rex was so busy trying to make heads or tails of that comment that he tripped over the clawed foot of a chair. Only Dora's quick reflexes saved him from falling on his face.

He couldn't help but hope she'd do equally well if they got into trouble in parliament. No, make than *when* they landed in hot water. Venturing into such an institution under false pretences was bad enough. Add on breaking and entering a private office space and Rex was envisioning them both being led away in manacles.

He had to put a stop to this nonsense. There was no way she'd thought this through. Even though she was easily the most clever person he'd ever had the honour to meet, still he doubted her ability to see this farce through without coming to harm.

Rex jerked to a halt, thereby forcing Dora to do the same. He spun her around until they were looking eye to eye.

"Dora, this is crazy. We'll never manage to pull this off. First, there's the guard at the gate who, in all likelihood, will turn us away. Even assuming we somehow make it past, we still have to make it through the public areas, up the stairs, down a private corridor within a restricted zone, and probably pick the lock on a door. And don't even get me started on getting out again!"

Dora waved off each of his reasons, appearing more and more blasé about the matter the longer he blustered on. "You injure me, Rex. After all our time together, have you no faith?"

Rex felt himself wavering and forced his mouth to turn into a disapproving frown. "I will not let you manipulate me, Theodora Laurent... or whatever your name really is."

"Fine, but I'm making note of this," Dora huffed. "First, as you said, is the guard. He will expect to see staff badges, like these." She pulled the pair of badges from her pocket and showed them to Rex. "Second, we'll have a letter explaining we're assigned to work on an upcoming private bill. That's where Cynthia comes in."

"Your housemaid?"

"She is so much more than a maid, darling boy. Have you learned nothing about my staff choices? No one is ever what they appear."

Rex wiped his hand over his face. "I've made a note for the future, but I still need you to fill in the gaps of my knowledge."

"As you know, Archie and Basil are expert pickpockets. When they mentioned their sister was in prison for forgery, I asked Audley to work his magic. It took little convincing for Cynthia to agree to work for the government, instead of serve time behind bars. Getting to be with her brothers was a bonus. She'll whip us up a suitable cover in no time."

Rex turned a blind eye to Dora's winsome smile. He wasn't ready to give in just yet. "That still leaves the door to the private office."

"Err, well yes, for that we have no choice but to pick the lock. As for getting out, we'll cross that bridge when we come to it. Honestly, once the hordes of staff, MPs and Lords descend on Westminster, it will be easy as pie to hide in plain sight and walk right back out again."

Rex gritted his teeth. Dora matched his move with a steely glare.

"Fine," he said, hissing the word through his grimace. "I want to trust you, but dammit woman, you don't make it easy on a chap."

Dora tossed back her head and laughed at his bald words. "Ironically, given the situation, the words of advice I'm about to offer you come from a Russian. Are you familiar with the work of Anton Chekhov?"

Rex shook his head, once again bewildered by Dora's unexpected shifts in conversation.

"No matter. I committed this quote to heart. Chekhov said, *'You must trust and believe in people or life becomes impossible.'* It is sage advice, and doubly so for anyone who chooses to spend part of their life gallivanting around with a spy."

Chapter 14
Snooping or sleuthing?

D ora didn't give Rex a moment to catch his breath, much less to identify all the flaws in her plan. Nonetheless, by the time they arrived at the front gates to Westminster, Big Ben chimed the last quarter bell before eight. This late in the year, the sun was barely over the horizon, but already Dora felt the urgency of time running short.

She elbowed Rex to jolt him from his pensiveness and handed him his badge. "Pin this to your coat and leave the talking to me." He did as she asked, giving her a moment for last checks.

Rex wore the off-the-rack suit Harris had procured for him. He'd added a fake moustache and beard to further hide his identity, and pulled the brim of his cap low to hide his eyes in its shadow.

Dora gave her own brunette wig a last tug and then pushed the thick glasses up her nose. The expression on Rex's face had finally shifted from abject terror to steely eyed determination. She took that as the sign to proceed.

A middle-aged man stood at the guard post. He'd pinned the arm of one sleeve up, identifying him as a veteran of the war.

It always made Dora's heart warm to see men such as him at work. Here, in Parliament, his presence was even more important. Every day, as the MPs and Peers walked past his station, they'd get a subtle reminder of the cost of their decisions. Right or wrong, the common man most often paid the price.

"Morning," the guard said. "You two are here early."

"Yes, we've got a timely assignment to complete." Dora fumbled with her handbag clasp while retrieving the forged letter.

The guard motioned for her to stop. "No need to explain. It seems today half the staff decided to come in before the rooster crowed. I sure wish someone would tell me what's going on."

Rex tensed up, and Dora spoke quickly to keep the guard from noticing. "Probably the backbenchers up to no good. We'd better get to work before this new mayhem throws our bill submission timelines into further chaos."

As expected, the guard chuckled and waved them through.

They reached the central hall without anyone raising the alarm. The guard had been right about the unexpected number of staff on site. However, everyone Dora saw seemed to be headed in the direction of the Commons offices and not toward the House of Lords. On any other day, Dora would have followed her gut instinct and investigated the situation. For now, however, it was the least of her worries.

When Rex stepped toward the Peers' corridor, Dora shot out a hand to stop him. "This way," she said, pointing at a door marked with a stairwell sign. "While I think it high unlikely we'll run into anyone we know, it's always better not to tempt fate."

Rex grimaced at how close he'd come to making an elementary mistake. In a barely audible voice, he asked, "How do you know your way around so well?"

"I took two of the official tours shortly after I arrived in London. With that as a foundation, I visited a third time under the guise of being a staffer."

"If you knew the lay of the land so well, why didn't his lordship give you this assignment?"

Dora paused on the stairwell landing. "Because I would have been as hamstrung as Murdoch. You, instead, have made great progress, specifically due to your ability to speak to the men in charge."

"And yet, here we are, sneaking around undercover..."

Dora didn't bother with a retort, in large part because Rex was right. What he was overlooking was that spy work rarely proceeded along a logical path. Dressing up and down, donning false identities, and blustering your way into off-limits spaces were all part of the job.

Although the stakes had increased exponentially since Rex started this assignment, the purpose remained the same. For the first time, he was getting a taste of spy life, with all its twists and turns. Dora didn't worry that he'd back out on her now, but she had her doubts about what he'd do when this assignment reached its end. She knew from experience that the first proper case marked the last turning point for new recruits. Either they embraced the life, or they abandoned it forever.

Although Rex was holding up well, particularly now while masquerading as staff in Westminster, Dora still didn't have a handle on what decision he'd make when all was said and done. She hated to admit it, but this bothered her a lot more than what she was letting on. She wanted Rex to stay on, to play the role of partner, and maybe someday take that role for real.

But worrying over the matter wasn't going to bring her any closer to an answer. When their route through the building delivered them to the door to the office shared by the leading

Liberal-leaning lords, Dora pushed her concerns aside and pulled a packet of tools from her handbag.

"Cover me," she whispered. The hallway was blessedly empty, but the clicking of her watch said it would not stay that way. The old-fashioned, Victorian lock on the door was a welcome discovery. Dora had plenty of experience with the likes. She picked two tools from her wallet and inserted the first one until she felt the latch lift. From there, it was simple enough to use the second tool to slide the latch over and unlock the door.

"How much longer are you going to take?" Rex asked, not daring to shift his gaze from monitoring the hallway.

"None. We're in." Dora got back to her feet and pushed the door open. Rex followed, hot on her heels, and closed the door behind them. Big Ben chimed the eight o'clock hour.

Light poured through the wide windows overlooking the River Thames, illuminating a space that looked closer to a smoking lounge than an office. A table for eight had a prominent position in the centre of the room, made of carved wood with a marble inset top. Built-in cabinets topped with book-filled shelves lined the walls. At the far end of the room, in front of the windows, Dora spied a seating area. The room designer had obviously ascribed to the "more is more" style of decor. Between the brocade upholstery and the heavily carved rosewood legs, the sofas and chairs didn't look so much comfortable as imposing.

The air was still, but held the scent of old cigar smoke. The room occupants likely spent hours here debating amongst themselves before presenting a united front to their fellow peers. Dora wished she could be a fly on the wall during such discussions. As a female, sitting in the House of Lords was not a possibility, regardless of her parentage or marital status. Only two women held seats in the Commons, at the other end of the building, the most recent having won a by-election following the death of the previous MP, who also happened to have been her husband.

The beginning of sick rage burned in her stomach, but Dora forced her mind to focus on the task at hand. The work she did now was as important as any member of parliament or peer of the realm. Moreover, she'd answered a calling that few might fill. There was no point despairing over what couldn't be, not when she was needed now.

Rex stood near the doorway, shifting from side-to-side as he burned his nervous energy. "Where do we start?"

"With the cabinets, I guess. You take the ones on the left, and I'll take these on the right. Grab anything that might be relevant. We need to act fast. I want to be out of here by the time Big Ben chimes the next quarter hour."

Rex gave a nod of confirmation and moved to the first cabinet in the line. Satisfied he was following orders, Dora did the same on the opposite side of the room.

The first cabinet she opened held bottles of Port and Scotch, a tray of crystal glasses, and a box of cigars. The tins of biscuits and chocolates coaxed a chuckle from her. No matter how old or how senior the man, life still required ready access to sweets.

Fortunately, the contents of the next cabinet proved more to her interest. Unfortunately, they were an utter mess. Mountains of papers haphazardly stacked had produced an avalanche of chaos. She was so dismayed; she shifted over to check the next cabinet in the line. To her horror, the situation grew even worse.

Dora stood and turned to see whether Rex was faring any better. Kneeling on the floor, she found him bending over a storage box. "Thank goodness!" she gasped. "Please tell me those documents are recent."

Rex's head snapped up at her voice. "Err, sorry. No can do. These are at least a decade old."

"Check the next one."

Rex replaced the lid on the box and slid it back into the cabinet. When he opened the next, he unveiled a similar scene, although this one had a stack of mid-sized boxes rather than a single large carton. He pulled the top one from the stack, tugged off the lid, and glanced inside. "These are more recent. Based on what I've seen so far, the documents appear to be stored according to a timeline. The ones nearest the door are the oldest, and each one is getting progressively closer to the present."

Rex's words did little to assuage Dora's mounting concern. She hurried to the fourth cabinet from the door on her side of the room, moving ever closer to the windows. There, she found an orderly stack of folders and envelopes. She filched one from the stack and flipped it open. The date on the top said December 1921. Her heart sank.

"Bad news, old chap. The information we seek is somewhere in the carnage of the two cabinets to my right." She watched as Rex's joyous expression gave way to horror when he got a good look at the state of the contents. "Right, we need a new plan. Stay put."

Dora leapt to her feet and hurried over to the door. She waved off Rex's question of where she was going. Slowly, she pulled the door open wide enough to peer through the gap. The corridor was still empty. Without hesitating another moment, she stepped into the hallway and began checking the names on the plaques beside the doors. She paid particular attention to those on the right side of the hall. Given their location, they were unlikely to have access to natural lighting. While that made them undesirable for office space, they were perfect for other purposes.

She hit pay dirt on the fourth door down. The knob twisted smoothly under her hand. The gas lighting in the corridor illuminated a narrow room filled with enshrouded statues. Dora took her torch from her pocket and switched it on, creating a narrow beam of light. She lifted the hem of the first item and bit back a laugh. The sheets weren't covering a statue. Instead, she saw the brass pendulum of a grandfather clock.

The dust tickled her nose, but she stifled a sneeze and declared the room perfect for their needs. This was exactly the type of space where one could sit uninterrupted for hours. She and Rex could search the papers methodically and return them when everyone took their lunch break. Instead of having only minutes, they'd have several hours.

She retraced her steps and found Rex sweating bullets in the office. She rattled off a set of instructions. "Grab as many of the papers as you can from this cabinet and follow me."

Within a few minutes, they'd relocated the papers into the storage room. To cover their tracks, they'd pulled older documents from the storage boxes and left them in a cluttered mess in the now empty cupboards. When Dora was satisfied that their temporary borrowing of the papers would go unnoticed at first glance, she locked the door to the Liberal office and scooted to their hiding place across the hall.

In the meantime, Rex had lit a gas lamp and cleared them a place to sit. Inside the storage room, the pair got to work. Silently, they sorted the papers into some semblance of order. After an hour, they had separated the private bills from the meeting minutes and had a towering stack of handwritten notes. The heavy wooden door prevented them from seeing outside, but enough voices leaked under the bottom to let them know the workday had begun in earnest.

"Don't think about it," Dora advised when Rex froze in place at running footsteps in the corridor. "No one knows we're here, and there is no reason why anyone would come into this room. Who would have an urgent need of a clock?"

Her words worked like a charm. Rex's shoulders settled

back into a relaxed position. They divvied the handwritten pages and began skimming them as quickly as the vague scribble permitted.

Anytime they saw the words Soviet, Russia, Chanak, Turkey, or Greece, they put the paper into Rex's briefcase. By the time they reached the bottom of the pile, Dora's stomach was growling and Rex kept rubbing his eyes. They were exhausted, but also hopeful. Together, they'd identified twenty pages that warranted closer inspection. The rest, they stacked up and tucked behind one of the covered clocks. It wasn't the best hiding place, but at least evidence of their thievery wouldn't be in plain sight.

With nothing left to do, the pair cleared two spaces against the wall. A bolt of fabric became a cushion, and with that, the two settled as best as they could.

"It will be easier to sneak away when everyone goes to lunch. We might as well catch a few winks," Dora suggested, knowing that was likely to happen no matter what she said. The madness of their night and morning demanded its toll.

"Lean your head on my shoulder," Rex said, shifting closer to her. Dora wasn't too proud to decline the offer. But she barely had time to close her eyes and inhale his masculine scent before a terrifying noise sent her senses to full alert.

She watched the doorknob twist under an unseen hand. Given there were over a thousand rooms in Westminster Palace, it was incredibly poor luck that someone was coming into this one.

Chapter 15
Thank goodness for Clark

A raven-haired man, as tall as the six-foot-high clock closest to the door, entered the room. The impeccable cut of his suit identified him as well-to-do. His fine leather boots matched a pair Rex had at home. That came as little surprise, given their valets patronised the same establishments.

As the wave of fear crashed against the shore of recognition, Rex couldn't stop himself from uttering the man's name.

"Clark?"

Lord Clark Kenworthy, for it was indeed him, searched the crowded storage room until he spotted the couple sitting against the wall. His eyes showed no recognition. It was then that Rex remembered he and Dora were still wearing their disguises. He swayed with indecision. Was he better off keeping to his assigned role, or coming clean? Clark was one of his oldest friends, but the circumstances were far from ordinary. For once, Rex hadn't a clue what to say to the man.

Dora solved the problem. She parted her lips, fluttered her lashes, and breathed Clark's name with a sigh of relief. "Why you darling, darling man! You had me half-terrified when you came in. We'd all but abandoned our hope that you were playing along with our little game."

Clark scrunched his brow and moved closer to the pair, peering at them intently. "Miss Laurent, is that you?"

"In the flesh," she replied, displaying a cavalier attitude as she climbed to her feet. "See, Rex! I told you Clark would be up for some fun."

Rex stood more slowly, still grappling to understand what Dora was doing. "You did?" He coughed to cover the question mark he'd accidentally included. "I mean, you did! Of course you did. You are always right. Now that Clark is here, the game is well and truly afoot."

Although Rex said all the right things, in truth, he was floundering to understand. What game? What message? What was afoot? As best as he could tell, the only thing they were playing fast and loose with was his reputation.

Clark wore a matching expression of bewilderment. The only one in the room who had any idea what they were doing was Dora.

Indeed, Dora was unfazed by being discovered wearing a disguise in a random storage room on the upper floor of Westminster. Based on her cool composure, one might think she did such things on a daily basis.

Rex gave Dora a pleading gaze and used his arm to nudge her forward, in a silent request for her to keep the lead.

Dora needed no further encouragement. She propped her hands on her hips and exclaimed, "You did get our note, didn't you? We dressed in disguises and snuck in. You were supposed to join us in playing the most delightful game of hide and seek. We've been waiting ages for you find us."

Despite having done nothing wrong, Clark flushed nonetheless. "I'm terribly embarrassed to admit that I did not.

Likely, it got lost in the mad shuffle of messages that have been flitting across London since late last night."

"Another game?" Dora asked, giving Clark her patented doe-eyed look.

"Shenanigans, for sure, but I'm afraid the current crisis is all too real. The Prime Minister resigned."

"What?" Dora and Rex cried in almost perfect unison.

"You haven't heard?" Clark replied, equally flummoxed.

Rex couldn't have been more surprised if the Prime Minister had walked into the storage room and announced his resignation in person. "But I saw the man last night at the Reform Club. I sat with him for nearly an hour and he never said a word!"

Clark shrugged. "Likely, he wasn't aware yet either. But this is hardly the place for a discussion on the matter. Can we adjourn somewhere else, ideally someplace with a fully stocked bar? I find myself to be parched."

Rex voiced his agreement, but Dora put up a hand to stop them.

"You're both welcome to come to mine, but before we rush off, I have a question. Clark, why did you come into this room if you weren't looking for us?"

Clark stared at the floor in an effort to hide his chagrined expression. "Don't tell anyone, but sometimes I come in here when I need a few minutes to myself. Today most certainly fits the bill. From the moment my butler awoke me with the news until a few minutes ago when I walked through that door, I haven't had two minutes in a row without someone clamouring to speak with me."

"I did not know you were such an important political figure," Dora said.

"That's just it!" Clark replied, throwing his hands into the air. "I am as politically insignificant as the man standing at your side."

"Wait, a minute—" Rex blurted, but Clark waved him off.

"It's true, man. We both know it. Other than inherited titles and dashing good looks, you and I have little to offer anyone hoping for political gain. But all that changes with a general election now looming on the horizon. The vote will be in less than a month. Every MP and challenger in the land has need of funds to make their case to the electorate. Until today, I'd thought refusing to declare affiliation with a party to be a particularly savvy move on my part. But instead of being on my own, I find myself sitting in the crosshairs of every man with a dream and an empty war chest."

Clark's face was flushed at this point. "This morning has been so bloody awful that I find myself willing to face a horde of marriage-minded mums if it means I can get out of here unscathed. Unless you have further questions, I suggest we make haste."

Clark turned around and marched to the door, not giving either Dora or Rex a chance to argue. Dora was happy enough to follow his lead, especially since Clark offered escape from their current predicament. But Rex had a concern.

"The papers," he whispered to Dora, pointing to the spot where they'd hidden them.

"Leave them. I doubt anyone is going to be looking for them today. I'll figure something out later."

Rex did as she said, but that didn't prevent him from feeling guilty. Even though there was nothing to connect him personally with the misplaced items, he was powerless to stop the niggling concern in the back of his mind. For once, however, he was going to have to adopt Dora's devil may care attitude. With so many people milling around the hallways, returning the papers to the Liberal meeting room was out of the question.

Without needing any instruction, Clark strode confidently along the corridor, leaving Dora and Rex to scuttle behind him, like the obedient staff that they were. Clark doffed his hat a time or two, but somehow avoided all attempts to engage him in conversation. With Dora and Rex following him, he had a ready-made excuse for why he couldn't stay.

"I'll come find you later," he promised a particularly persistent MP. "I must meet with my staff first and review what funds I can provide before I make any promises. I'm sure you understand."

The MP grimaced, but backed off, having no idea that he had not one, but two lords before him. If he'd had any idea of Rex's identity, he could have asked for a blank cheque. Rex kept his gaze focused on the floor and hurried past, counting his blessing and cursing the entire situation in equal measure.

After an eternity spent descending stairwells and winding their way through the maze of corridors, the trio emerged into the midday sun.

"Your car?" Clark asked Rex.

"We came by taxi." Rex pointed to the line of ubiquitous black vehicles waiting outside the gate. "I suggest we avail ourselves of the same form of transport again. We can sneak into Theodora's home and leave everyone else to assume you're still here."

"Capital idea!" Clark answered. He walked to the front of the line and opened the car door for Dora to enter. Once they were all inside, Dora rattled off her address and they were standing on her doorstep in no time flat.

Harris opened the front door and expressed no surprise at finding the unlikely group waiting for entry. He ushered them, collecting their coats, hats, and, in Rex's case, briefcase. Dora directed Harris to show Clark into her drawing room before disappearing upstairs to change into something more appropriate. Rex excused himself to remove the fake beard and moustache from his face and promised to join Clark in a few moments.

Once again looking like himself, Rex found himself surprisingly at home playing the man of the house. He knew where in the drawing room Dora kept her best whiskey and glasses, and he even had a favourite chair.

Clark, ever eagle-eyed, arrived at a similar conclusion. "I wasn't aware you and Theodora were so serious. Watching you now, I'd guess this was as much your home as hers."

Rex raised and discarded a variety of replies before opting on the simplest. "What can I say? In my shoes, would you spend your free time elsewhere?"

"Unfortunately, no. I would not."

Rex handed Clark a glass and took the chair opposite him. "Why unfortunately?"

Clark chuckled. "I keep hoping you'll find something else to interest you, and open the door for another man to make a go at attracting Theodora's attention."

"Do I get any say in the matter?" Dora asked as she came through the door. Dressed once again in her own clothes, with her reddish-blonde locks brushed until they shone, she was quite the picture.

"You're the only one with any say in the matter," Clark replied, without missing a beat. "Why you let Bankes-Fernsby here turn your head is beyond me."

Dora angled her steps to walk behind the wing chair where Rex was sitting. She dragged her fingertips across his shoulders before coming around to prop herself on the armrest beside him. "I'd be happy to list his positive traits, but I'm afraid it won't make for a pleasant conversation for you, dear Clark. What say you? Shall we turn our talk to more pressing matters — namely, the resignation of the Prime Minister?"

When Clark agreed, Rex fought off the desire to lean closer to Dora's perfumed form, and instead forced himself to pay attention.

"This story actually begins in a building a few doors down from the Reform Club," Clark said. "The Tories had a meeting of the minds at their favourite establishment. From what I understand, tempers ran hot, voices were raised, but eventually they landed on the same side of the issue of the day. Namely, they all agreed that Lloyd George was no longer fit to lead the coalition. They had enough votes to ensure a ballot of no confidence and sent a note to alert Lloyd George to his change in fortune."

"That must have been the note he received while I was sitting with him!" Rex gasped. "If only I'd stuck around a while longer."

"If you had, I doubt you'd have enjoyed the experience. Rumour has it that his reply was volatile and immediate. He resigned as Prime Minister and told the Tories he had no need of their support. He plans to put the decision into the hands of the voters and form a new government on his terms, not theirs."

"Is that likely to happen?" Dora asked.

Clark tossed back the remainder of his drink and grimaced as the alcohol burned his throat. "Pardon my choice of wording, but Lloyd George is a darned fool. The Tories and the Labour party are crowing in satisfaction. We can't be certain until the election is past, but I suspect the Liberals will find themselves on the outside looking in, instead of running the show."

Dora was stunned. Just when she thought she had a firm grasp on the political situation, this storm came through, shifting the sands until the landscape was unrecognisable. "If you are right about all this, why would Lloyd George resign?"

"Because he is pompous. He's been butting heads with the leading Tories for months now. The coalition was bound to fall, eventually. This matter in Turkey only hastened the timeline. So there you have it." Clark stared morosely into his empty glass. "We may have avoided international conflict, but the post-war consensus has reached its end. The political parties will return to ways of old, jostling for position and fighting over every crumb of power."

Even Dora's shoulders sank at Clark's answer. "What will you do now?" she asked. "Will you pick a side?"

Clark sighed and gave his head a shake. "No. Now, more than ever, independent-minded men such as myself and the other cross-benchers will become critical to ensuring some kind of check and balance. As long as there are at least a few of us willing to buck the status quo and force everyone to the negotiating table, there is hope that we can avoid the government rushing headfirst into terrible decisions."

Chapter 16
A new dilemma

C lark accepted Dora's gracious invitation to stay for lunch. Although the conversation turned to other matters, Dora's mind remained firmly engaged in the current predicament.

Was it only last night that Dora had sent Rex off to dinner with Lord Newbury? If she had an ounce of foresight, Dora would have instructed him to remain firmly fixed to Newbury's side so he could watch the matters play out.

Unfortunately, neither soothsaying nor fortune-telling were within her wheelhouse. Although she had an exceptionally keen mind and plenty of experience at predicting waves of change, this one had escaped her.

Dora did not need to ask the question to find out why. Instead of worrying about the larger political ramifications, she'd been entirely focused on finding the source of the false intelligence, and with it, the identity of Murdoch's murderer.

Now, just when she needed his insights the most, Lord Audley was missing. The timing of his kidnapping could not be a coincidence. It had to be related to the larger events of the prior evening. It was exactly as Clark had said. With the political world in a state of upheaval, the support of the independent cross-benchers could mean the difference between success and total failure, particularly for the smaller parties like the Liberals and Labour.

If Lord Audley were here, he would almost certainly be gathering men such as Clark for discussions and debates. Although he was one man, his presence would make a difference. Someone needed him to be out of the way. But who?

By the time Clark, Rex, and Dora finished their coffee and dessert, Dora had not arrived at a conclusion. Exhaustion had her mind feeling as though it were walking through treacle, her thoughts too slow to form any connection. Unfortunately, she had to wait for Clark to leave before she could get any rest. It took all of her skills at simpering and smiling to mask her annoyance with their lingering houseguest. If she wasn't still grateful that Clark had helped them get away from Westminster and shared all the news, she'd have shown him to the door a half-hour earlier.

It was Rex's yawn which finally caught Clark's attention. "My word! How long were you in that storage room waiting?"

"Since dawn," Rex replied, seeing no point in keeping that a secret. "And that was after we spent the night painting the town red. I'm sorry to admit it, but I find myself flagging."

"Let me get out of your hair so you can get some rest. Both of you," Clark added, eyeing the dark shadows under Dora's eyes. "I hate to say it, but I'm afraid I'll have little time for follies until the election is behind us. Rex, I'd heard through the grapevine that you were interested in testing your hand at politics. Take my advice and sit out until the dust settles. There is nothing to be gained from drawing attention to yourself right now."

"Quite right," Rex agreed, rising from his chair. "At the moment, I'm exhausted enough that having a month-long lie in sounds like just the thing. Give us a ring when you are ready to resume your footloose and fancy free ways, old chap."

Clark promised to do just that and a few minutes later, left via the front door. Dora barely had time to rise from her chair before Harris darkened the dining room doorway.

"I've prepared rooms for both of you upstairs. You're to go straight up and have a lie down while you can still make your way there on your own."

"But Harris, Audley is missing and we have a lead. Now's not the time for a nap," Dora argued, albeit half-heartedly. A nap sounded decidedly attractive, even if a poor use for her time.

Harris put one hand on his hip and used the other to point upstairs. "Your argument would have been more believable if you hadn't punctuated it with a yawn. You're definitely not in a fit state to do Audley any good. Now go, before Inga gets back from his lordship's home and takes a rolled up paper to the back of your legs."

Dora's eyes widened as the threat hit home. She took Rex's arm and directed him to the stairs.

"Inga wouldn't really swat you, would she?"

Dora stopped in the middle of the stairs to give Rex a deadpan expression. "Do you want to find out?"

Rex did not. Neither did Dora. They said goodnight in the corridor and entered their designated rooms on either side. Within minutes, they were both fast asleep.

When Dora awoke several hours later, it was to find Inga's face inches above her own. She bit back a yelp and earned a smile from her best friend.

"Time to rise and shine, your sleepiness. Lord Audley isn't going to save himself."

Inga's reminder worked better than a cattle prod at getting Dora out of the bed. She didn't even grumble while getting dressed, although she slurped greedily at the waiting cup of coffee. The long nap had gone a long way toward restoring her sanity, but she was still running at a deficit.

"Is Rex awake yet?"

"Harris is getting him up now. His valet sent over a change of clothes. I expect he'll be down shortly. There's a cold buffet laid out in the dining room. Help yourself to some food and then we'll put our heads together to determine what to do next."

On any other day, Dora would have chafed at taking orders. But today, still groggy from the afternoon spent sleeping, she relinquished her need to be in control and let someone else do the thinking. She trundled downstairs and helped herself to the salads, breads, and continental meats and cheeses.

By the time their bellies were full, both Dora and Rex were thinking clearly enough to dive back into their investigation. Cynthia, the maid, and her brothers, the footmen, made quick work of clearing the dining room. Harris brought in the documents they'd found at Murdoch's flat and spread them across the tabletop. Rex and Dora added the ones they'd borrowed from the Liberal common room. Inga finished the exercise with the addition of Audley's secret files.

There were so many papers it was impossible to know where to start.

Dora decided to deal with the mess they'd left behind in Westminster first. "Harris, could you send Archie or Basil to Westminster after dark, so they can return the remainder of the documents we temporarily relocated?"

"Of course. They can masquerade as part of the cleaning crew." Harris excused himself to pass along the message and was back in a thrice.

"How do you want to tackle this?" Inga asked Dora, waving her hand over the piles of papers.

Dora surveyed the papers strewn across the table. Seeing them all spread out drove home the gargantuan size of their task. As Molière once said, *"The greater the obstacle, the more glory in overcoming it."* Nothing would be more glorious than bringing Lord Audley home safe. Dora decided to keep that end goal in mind, instead of worrying so much about all the things still standing in their way.

"We're going to solve this as a team. Inga, you take Audley's papers. Harris, stick with Murdoch's files, and Rex, since you're already familiar with them, you take on the Liberal party notes." Dora waited for her friends and allies to position themselves around the table accordingly. "Inga, we'll start with you. Check Audley's papers to see when was the first date he made a note of the rumour about the Soviets."

Inga flipped through the pages until she located the first mention. "Here it is. The date is September twenty-fifth."

"Excellent. Rex, can you pull all documents dated between September twentieth and the twenty-fifth? I can't imagine Lloyd George sat on the intelligence for long."

Rex flipped through the pages until he found the correct dates. "Whoever took these notes needs a lesson in penmanship, but I think this word here is Soviet. What do you think?" Rex walked over and handed the paper to Dora.

"Yes, that's Soviet, all right. There's even a specific mention of Lenin and the Turks." Dora quickly skimmed the page, searching for a list of meeting attendees. "Lloyd George and Churchill were there, as were St Cecil and Sutherland."

"Lord Sutherland? The Tory?" Inga scrunched her brow. "Do the meeting notes mention anything about Sutherland's opinion on the matter?"

"No, not that I can see," Rex said, scanning the page again. "It appears this was the first time he floated the rumour past the Prime Minister. Perhaps Sutherland was keeping his cards close to his chest until he had to conduct his own investigation into the matter. Again and again, we keep coming back to the same individual. I must speak with St Cecil. If he has Audley hidden away somewhere, I'll find him."

Rex appeared ready to walk out the door and demand an immediate meeting, but Dora was still unconvinced. She held up a hand to stop him.

"Before you rush off, answer me this. How is St Cecil benefiting from passing along false intelligence?"

"Err, what?" Rex blurted.

"Think about it. Audley always has a reason for his actions. In this particular case, he was trying to avert a war. But what was the aim of the other player in this spy game? It can't be going to war, because even the risk of Soviet involvement wasn't enough to convince the other political parties to support Lloyd George's plan. As for political gain, we heard what Clark said. Lloyd George ended up looking so bad that he had to resign. The Liberal party is likely going to take a significant hit at the polls. Unless something major happens between now and election day, the party will end up out of power for at least the next election cycle, if not longer."

Rex pulled out a chair from the table and slumped into it. He covered his face with his hands and groaned in despair. "I want to argue with you, but you make it darn near impossible when you assail me with impeccable logic. If I were a Liberal today, I'd be hanging my head in shame."

"So, who's happy?" Inga asked, glancing from Dora to Rex and back again.

Dora stared off into the distance and considered the

question. Only one answer came to mind. "The Tories. In one night, they usurped control of the government and ousted Lloyd George from his perch as Prime Minister." Dora turned to Rex and added, "I know we crossed them off our suspect list, but we made a mistake. Sutherland and Godfrey are back in consideration. They have vast political experience, their own networks, and direct access to the Prime Minister."

"Yes, but they are also ardently outspoken about the topic of Russian interference. Sutherland has outwardly called the PM a fool, on more than one occasion. Godfrey has only been willing to admit that the Soviets might be a threat someday in the future. But not now." Rex shook his head. "That said, you're the expert here. Who am I to say that you're wrong? I'm afraid I don't have enough experience with either of the men to say whether they are capable of outmanoeuvring the PM to this degree. This is why we so desperately need to find Audley."

Dora launched into step, pacing back and forth beside the table. "I suspect this is exactly why someone kidnapped Audley off the street last night. Think again about the timing. The Tories sent their message to Lloyd George late in the evening. You were there to see it delivered. Two hours later, Audley is kidnapped. The Tories were the only ones with enough information to pull off a heist at that level. If I were making a run for control of the government, Lord Audley would absolutely be someone I'd want out of the way."

"How do we get him back?" Rex asked in a low tone. "And please, don't look at me. Dining and smoking cigars with the political elite is one thing. I am not experienced enough to do more than that. There's too much about Godfrey and Sutherland that remains unknown."

Dora halted in her tracks and spun to face Rex. Her face was strangely pale, but her steely expression left no room for argument. "We're going to need an insider — someone we can trust unconditionally."

Inga shifted in her chair, furiously shaking her head. "No, Dora. Audley wouldn't ask this of you. We'll find another way."

Dora inhaled and held in the breath, digging deep until she was strong enough to hold on to her resolve. "I don't have a choice. We're going to have to ask the Duke of Dorset for help."

Chapter 17
An identity revealed

I n his early days of training, Rex had often felt like an outsider. Dora, Inga, and Harris had such a long history of working together, they often finished one another's sentences. One had only to mutter half a phrase for the other two to intuit exactly what one needed.

But over the past six months, he'd grown accustomed to their jokes and patter. He'd memorised how Dora took her tea, and which magazines Inga pretended to hate but secretly loved. For the life of him, however, he did not understand why Dora's statement warranted such heartfelt expressions of concern from Inga and Harris. They acted as though Dora had suggested contacting the devil himself and not a peer of the realm.

Six months ago, Rex would have sat back and waited for someone to fill in the gaps, or hoped to do it himself in time. But not now, and not on a matter of this level of importance. Especially given the little they'd told him of Audley's relationship with the Duke. Those two were hardly friends.

He cleared his throat to get everyone's attention. "Why would you ask Lord Audley's arch-nemesis for help? And furthermore, why would he offer it?"

Inga and Harris carefully avoided his gaze.

Dora gulped. Rex had the suspicion that she was deciding how much to tell him.

"Yes, they are rivals, but it is a rivalry born out of respect for one another. The Duke of Dorset would not do anything to actually harm Lord Audley."

Rex wanted to follow her logic, but it was so full of holes, he couldn't make it across. "Even assuming that is true, we'd be asking the Duke to go against members of his own political party. And how much are you going to tell him about the situation? Does the Duke know Lord Audley oversees a network of spies?"

Dora swayed on her feet, clearly uncomfortable being the subject on Rex's inquisition. "I'm fairly certain the Duke has some idea our network exists. He obviously knows Lord Audley has access to sensitive intelligence."

Rex couldn't believe his ears. From day one, Dora and Lord Audley both had drilled the necessity of absolute secrecy into his head. He was required to remain quiet about his link to his lordship, and not to hint that Theodora was something other than what she appeared.

Now, Dora stood before him, suggesting they throw all that training to the wind. Not only that, but to do so with someone potentially on the wrong side of the matter. He had no idea what had got into her. Seeing Lord Audley kidnapped before their very eyes must have shocked her to her core. Either that, or the sleep deprivation had driven her mad.

No matter what, Rex had to save Dora from herself. He crossed his arms across his chest and stood firm in his reply. "No. I will not do it. There has to be a better way. If we sit here long enough, we'll come up with it. If we really and truly need help from a political insider, we can call Clark. He's definitely not involved."

Inga and Harris exchanged glances over the top of the dining table. Neither spoke out against his suggestion.

Dora, however, was having none of it, despite being obviously ill at ease with her own plan. Although she shook her head no, she kept opening and closing her hands into fists by her side. If she gnawed at her lip any harder, it was sure to bleed.

Whom else might they ask? Rex cast his mind back to FitzClarence's soiree. Who had been in the game room watching the two conservative lords debate? The only person he remembered clearly was the Duke of Dorset, and that was only because the two men had chatted.

Rex remembered then how their conversation had started. "What about the Duke's son Benedict? He lent us a hand during the investigation into Freddie's death. Let's approach him instead."

"Benedict will not help us this time around." Dora's statement left no room for argument.

Rex goggled. "Why not? I'm not being obtuse, Dora, but I really do not understand. You say we can only trust the Duke of Dorset, even though he is no friend of Lord Audley, but cannot ask his own son for help?"

Dora sucked air in between her teeth. "Benedict isn't going to help us, because it is not in his best interest to do so this time around. Last time, I was able to convince him otherwise. I have little hope of doing the same again. Not while he has the upper hand."

"That's the truth," Inga muttered. "Fine mess you find yourself in, and even worse, it is one entirely of your own making."

Dora flushed and dropped her head in shame.

Rex could stand it no longer. With this strange display of behaviour, everything Rex knew to be true about this world crumbled to ash. Audley, who had always seemed unbeatable, was gone. Dora, who had the confidence to bluster her way through any situation, was staring shamefacedly at the carpet.

And Rex still struggled to make sense of it.

Part of him wanted to throw his hands in the air and leave them all to clean up the mess. If whatever was bothering Dora was so bad, he had no hope of solving it on his own.

But there was still one cold hard fact he had to face. If he got up now and walked out the front door, Dora would never let him back in again. No amount of apologising or pleading would make up for the fact that he had abandoned her in a moment of need.

He had a decision to make. Was he going to stand beside Dora, come hell or high water?

Or was he going to take the easy way out, and return to his old, pointless life where his only aspiration was fathering more boys to carry on the family name?

He'd spent six months training for this decision. He thrust himself to his feet and strode around the table to take Dora in his arms. When she refused to lift her head, he tucked his hand under her chin and nudged her head until their eyes met.

"Theodora Laurent, I am your partner in all this. I may not have been here as long as Inga and Harris, but that doesn't lessen my commitment to our shared cause, nor to you. I've been content to let you keep your secrets, but whatever this one is can no longer remain between us. I am asking you to trust me, the way I trust you."

Dora narrowed her gaze and searched his face for any hint of subterfuge. Rex held perfectly still, not even daring to blink. He had no secrets from her.

For a long moment, he was sure she would refuse. But then her expression shifted. Her pinched mouth smoothed into a flat line. Her eyes opened wider, and her gaze softened. More importantly, he felt her fingers grip tight onto his shirt, holding him in place. Whatever she had to say next would not come easy.

She took a deep breath, releasing it slowly while she chose her words. "I know we can trust the Duke of Dorset because I have known him my entire life."

Rex didn't let up. "There's more, isn't there?"

Dora nodded. "Benedict and I have engaged in games of one-upmanship since I was old enough to walk."

"How can that be? You two gave no sign!"

Dora shushed Rex. "I kept a secret of his in exchange for him keeping mine. It was beneficial for both of us to collaborate together. Unfortunately, that is no longer true. It hasn't been since the night we went to the party at the FitzClarences."

"The night you had to sneak off because you ran into someone from your past." Rex didn't wait for her to reply. "It wasn't the Duke, because he was in the same room as I. Nor Benedict, although I believe he was also in attendance. So, who was it?"

Dora closed her eyes and whispered the response. "My mother. I saw my mother."

Whatever Rex expected her to say, this wasn't it. He was so shocked that he dropped his hold and stumbled backward. All the pieces were on the table. He had only to figure out how they fit together.

Dora, who Audley said was as highborn as Rex.

Benedict and the Duke, who'd known Dora for her entire life.

There was only one way all of those things could be true.

"You're a Cavendish," he blurted. "A cousin? Niece?"

Dora shook her head. "I never meant for you to find out this way. Nor for them to see me this soon. Yet, here we are, with lives more important than my own on the line. So, I must tell you my truth. I believe daughter and sister are the words you seek. "

Dora dropped her arms and straightened her shoulders. She lifted her head into the imperious expression of a titled woman born to a family of wealth and privilege. "My name is Lady Dorothy DeVere, née Cavendish, Dowager Viscountess of Lisle."

Rex's mouth dropped and hung open. Not only Cavendish but also DeVere? A man's face flashed through his memory. He'd seen the man hearty and hale, and only hours later, had witnessed his murder. The question tumbled from his lips.

"Lucien?" he asked. "You and Lucien?"

"He was my husband, even if only for a single night. Now you understand why I was so invested in identifying his killer all those years ago. Audley offered me the chance to live a different life, one unencumbered by familiar obligations and societal expectations. I leapt at the opportunity and convinced Inga to join me. Since then, Audley assured my family I was safe, while never letting on to what I was really doing."

"But then, why are you here?"

"Because I missed them." Dora shrugged as though she didn't believe it either. "I spent half a decade hightailing it from one end of the earth to another. The more confident I became in my new identity, the greater my desire to share it with those I love. I cajoled Audley into letting me return to London for a short sabbatical, and I've been biding my time before coming clean with my parents."

"Benedict didn't tell them?" Rex was aghast. In Benedict's shoes, he'd never keep a secret that enormous to himself.

"Benedict has no idea of what I really do. He thinks the same thing as the rest of the world. He didn't tell my parents, because he feared their reaction. If anyone was going to bear the brunt of their anger, it was to be me."

While Rex processed her explanation, Inga and Harris rose from their seats and moved around to flank Dora. All together, they presented a united front.

It was Harris who spoke. "Now you understand the importance of keeping Dora's real identity a secret. If anyone discovered she was a spy for Audley and the daughter of Lord Cavendish, they would have the power to cripple both men in one fell swoop. Dora may not need to hear you say the words, but I do. Do you swear to keep this information a secret for the rest of your life? I don't ask this question lightly. So few people had access to the information that it would be immediately obvious who let this slip."

Rex did not hesitate. "I swear to protect this information with my life. For all our sakes. I recognise the risks to all of us. If I spoke out about Dora, I'd put all of us in the same line of fire."

"Good." Harris offered Rex a hand. "Welcome to our inner circle."

Inga's smile stretched from ear to ear. "I believe I speak for all of us when I say I need a drink. Harris, help me get the glasses."

Harris and Inga left Rex and Dora alone in the dining room. Rex shuffled awkwardly, suddenly unsure of how to interact with the woman standing in front of him.

Dora spoke and her voice trembled. "Do you hate me?"

"Hate you?" Rex's head reared back. "Why on earth would you think such a thing?"

"Because I lied to you. I should have told you sooner. It wasn't that I didn't trust you..."

"Then why did you wait?"

Dora's mouth twisted into a wry grin. "Because I was scared that you wouldn't find me nearly as interesting once you learned the truth."

Rex engulfed her in a hug. "You silly, silly woman! Hearing

your full lineage rattle off your tongue only raised you in my estimation. And that's saying a lot, given how high I held you from the start."

Harris harrumphed from the doorway and the pair split apart like guilty lovers caught in an embrace. "Here are your glasses. Inga will pour."

The four raised their crystal whiskey glasses in a toast and drank deeply, allowing the alcohol to dull the edges of their earlier stress.

"How do we do this? Do you want me to escort you to the Cavendish home?" Rex asked when they were all seated and relaxed.

"No! Theodora Laurent can hardly be seen waltzing up their front steps. Tongues would wag for days. Same goes for inviting them here. There is, however, a third option which will suit us nicely."

Rex thought for a moment, but the answer remained out of reach. "Well, go on then. Tell me."

"You can host them... or rather, your grandmother. After all, no one refuses an invitation from the Dowager Duchess of Rockingham."

Rex didn't quibble over her statement, but he did have a question. "But won't my grandmother ask why?"

Dora gave a half-shrug of apology. "Err, not exactly. She has a reputation for having an almost preternatural awareness of all of London's gossip... and I can attest that it is is well deserved. Your grandmother figured out my true identity the moment I set foot in her drawing room."

Chapter 18
Meet the parents

Dora checked her reflection in a gilt-framed mirror hanging in the drawing room of the Dowager Duchess of Rockingham. She smoothed a loose curl back into place and fluffed the bottom of her fashionable bob. Reassured everything was as close to perfect as it could be, she hesitated to move away from the mirror.

Dora didn't notice Theodora Laurent's famously thick lashes, nor the vibrant red colour of her lipstick.

It was the reflection of her emerald eyes that caused her to still. Cavendish eyes, her mother always said. Dora might dye her hair and play with make-up, but there was nothing she could do to disguise her eyes.

In truth, she'd never wanted to try. Every time she looked in the mirror, she saw her brother Wills staring back at her. Forever young, just one more casualty of the horrors of the Somme. Dora carried his spirit with her everywhere she travelled, living adventures enough for them both.

Would her mother understand why she'd disappeared all those years ago, with hardly more than a letter every Christmas to reassure everyone she was still alive? Dora wasn't sure. It was that doubt that had driven her to keep her distance since she'd arrived in London. Never mind her plans to reconnect with family. For a woman who never said no to a risk, she'd developed a distinct fear of failure when it came to the test of seeing her mother.

"Take this," Inga said, startling Dora from her reverie. She passed Dora a cocktail. "Facing one's fears head-on can leave a bitter taste in the mouth. This gin and tonic should help wash it away."

"Ahh, yes. Dutch courage. It hasn't failed me yet." Dora raised her glass in a toast. "Does my dress look okay?"

Inga took a half step back and surveyed her friend from head to toe. "Flamboyant enough for Theodora to wear, but with a high enough neckline that your mother shouldn't swoon. I couldn't have chosen better myself. Although it would look a lot better if you ceased drying your palms on the skirt."

Dora froze mid-motion and forced her hand to slide upward until she propped it on her hip. "I can't imagine what you mean by that."

Inga's only reply was a pair of raised eyebrows and a highly skeptical slant to her mouth. The entrance of the Dowager Duchess herself into the drawing room saved Dora from having to come up with something else.

It was said that even the royal family was hesitant to cross Rex's grandmother. Despite her silvered hair and sedate walk, one only had to glance at the Dowager's proud carriage and impeccable style to know they were in the presence of a grande dame. Dora had never been more thankful to have remained firmly on the Dowager's good side.

"Miss Laurent, aren't you the very picture of youthful beauty?" the Dowager gushed. "And Miss Kay, you are equally stunning in blue. You simply must make a habit of wearing that shade more often."

"Yes, it makes for a pleasant change from the blacks and greys she prefers so she can hide in the shadows," Dora replied. She crossed the room and air-kissed Rex's grandmother's cheeks. "I can't say thanks enough for hosting this dinner on such short notice."

"My dear, it is I who is grateful. I'd have paid good money to be a fly on the wall for your family reunion, and instead, you delivered a front-row seat. Now, do you have any last requests before they arrive?"

Dora frowned. "Last, as in you believe that my mother may kill me?"

The Dowager pretended to be scandalised. "In my dining room? Why, she'd end up ostracised from society. I meant where would you like us to sit?"

A loud knock sounded from the foyer before Dora replied. She noted the measured footsteps of Sheffield, the butler, followed by the scrape of the front door swinging open. Where was Rex? He had promised to stay close, but here she was, without him in sight.

Then, his baritone voice welcomed their guests. He greeted her father and brother in a loud enough tone for her to be forewarned of their arrival. For a half-second, Dora feared her mother had declined to show up. But then, she heard a clear mezzo-soprano introducing herself to Rex.

Rex led them to the drawing room. He lingered in the doorway, his eyes searching the room until he spotted Dora. She gave a single nod. Ready or not, this was happening.

Benedict came through next, his mouth twisted into an evil grin when he spied his wayward sister. It was reassuring that he showed no surprise at Dora's presence. Dora had trusted that by now, her mother would have uncovered everything there was to know about Theodora Laurent, and would have recognised the Dowager Duchess's invitation for what it was.

A chance to dine with her daughter.

Her father came next. That threw Dora off-guard. She'd expected her mother, but apparently her father was taking no chances. His expression was impassive as he stared at her, taking her measure. Dora forced her back to remain straight under the weight of his gaze.

Finally, Dora's mother came through the door. She wore a gown of watered blue silk and accented it with the family diamond and sapphire jewels around her neck and wrists. She'd twisted her dark hair into a chignon. Despite the differences in their hair and eye colour, there was little question that she was Dora's mother. They shared the same eye shape and cheekbones, and their figures were similarly slim.

The Duchess of Dorset's blue eyes widened, and she gasped almost imperceptibly.

It was the gasp that proved Dora's undoing. Despite everything she'd promised herself about remaining strong and giving her mother space, the little girl who still lived inside her took full control. Dora thrust her drink in Inga's direction, barely pausing long enough to make sure she had it, and then she all but ran to her mother.

Adaline Cavendish, Duchess of Dorset, opened her arms wide and pulled her daughter into a tight embrace.

Dora sniffled, powerless against the tumultuous wave of rightness she felt in that moment.

"Oh, my precious girl. It really is you!" Adaline loosened her hold enough that she could get a good look at Dora.

"Of course, it's me, Mama. Who else could convince the Dowager Duchess to play hostess to a notorious femme fatale?"

"I'd like to think I had some role in this," Rex said. "I live here, too."

"Son, in moments like this one, it's best to let the women

take all the credit." Dora's father eyes shone with pride. "Now come here, daughter of mine, and give me a hug."

Dora didn't need to be asked twice. She untangled herself from her mother and did as her father asked. His scent was exactly like she remembered, of pipe smoke and the cologne her mother preferred. After a long moment, he let her loose and gave her a stern frown. "You are still in trouble, young lady, even if we are delighted to see you safe and whole."

Benedict spluttered, getting everyone's attention. His face was flushed in anger at his parents' thoroughly unexpected response to seeing his sister. "That's it? That's all you're going to say after five years of silence?"

The Duke shifted awkwardly. "We weren't completely in the dark about your sister's whereabouts. Or rather, I should say we knew she lived and had a darned good reason for what she'd done. Although," he turned to glare at Dora, "did you have to send your messages through Lord Audley? You know how much that man enjoys getting my goat."

"Why else do you think I approached him?" Dora said, without an ounce of regret. "Lord Audley is, in fact, the reason we're gathered here."

"Dora, you promised we'd save the business talk for after our meal," the Dowager Duchess admonished. "Now, please. Finish the introductions so the men can escort us through to supper."

The party was small enough that it only took a moment to complete the intros. The Dowager asked Rex to accompany her, leaving Dora's parents arm-in-arm. That left Benedict with the choice of either his sister or Inga. He chose the latter, making sure to sniff in disapproval while he walked past Dora.

His slight rolled off Dora's shoulders like water off a duck. Nothing her older brother said or did would burst her happiness over finally being reconciled with her parents.

Out of deference to the private nature of their

conversations, the staff had arranged to serve the meal family style on the Dowager Duchess's impressive dining table. Sheffield stayed long enough to pour wine and ensure all was in place, and then even he excused himself from the room. He closed the doors behind him, leaving the small group free to speak openly with one another.

Over dinner, Dora's parents took turns asking about Dora's adventures. They expressed their thanks to Inga for having stayed by their daughter's side, no matter where life had taken her. Even Benedict unwound long enough to express his astonishment at her African safari.

"You mean to say that all the rumours about you and your exploits are true?" he asked, aghast.

"Most of them," Dora clarified, flashing a sly grin. "Far be it from me to separate the fiction from the fact, especially not when the end story only adds to my charm."

Benedict rolled his eyes, causing his mother to smother a chuckle behind her hand. "Egads, you really haven't changed a bit. You always were a cheeky little thing."

"Cheeky or not, I'm just happy she's here," Adaline said, cutting in before her son could say something worse. "Although, if you make me wait another half a decade to see your face, I will take you over my knee, young lady."

Inga cackled at Dora's mother's threat, earning herself a light rap on the arm from Dora.

Eventually, after partaking of food and drink, the conversation hit a natural lull. The Dowager suggested she, Inga, and the Duchess adjourn to her sitting room for a game of cards, leaving Dora, Rex, and the others to discuss business matters in the drawing room. Benedict, still fuming that his sister hadn't got more flack, chose that moment to make his departure.

It took but a few minutes for everyone to make their way to

their assigned locations in the house. In the drawing room, Dora availed herself of the silk-upholstered sofa. Dora's father stationed himself across from his daughter. Rex moved to sit beside Dora, but a well-timed glower from the Duke had him rethinking his choice. Instead, he settled into a nearby wingback.

Sheffield poured tawny Port and offered a light to the men. He left the decanter on the sideboard and promised to return later with tea and coffee.

Dora's father took a puff on his cigar and turned to exhale away from the others. When he faced front again, he speared his daughter with a searing gaze. "All right, Dora. As much as it pains me, I know you didn't call us here for a family reunion."

"That was partially my reason," Dora argued, but her father held up a hand to forestall her from saying more.

"You mentioned something earlier about Lord Audley. Where is he? I must admit, I had wondered why he was absent from Westminster today. I'd hoped he was licking his wounds after the coalition collapsed, even though a retreat of any kind would be out of character. Start from the beginning and tell me how I can help."

Chapter 19
A request for aid

As agreed, Rex led the conversation. "Someone kidnapped Lord Audley off the street two nights ago."

Dora's father reared backwards. "You're sure of this?"

"Yes, sir. We saw it with our own eyes."

"You're telling me that the Duke of Montagu is missing and you have somehow kept this quiet?" The Duke of Dorset stared at Rex and Dora. "I'm hardly his biggest fan, but even I would sound the alarm at such news. You two had better have a darned good reason for remaining mum until now."

"We do, Father, and we'll take you through everything. But we wanted you to understand the level of seriousness of the situation from the start."

Dora's father was skeptical, but Dora reached over to rest her hand on top of his leg. He sighed and nodded for Rex to continue.

"This chain of events began a month ago, with the rumour about the Turks allying with the Soviets. This intelligence was patently false, but Audley couldn't convince Lloyd George to let it go. The more he argued against it, the harder the Prime Minister dug in his heels. Audley had to go to great lengths to prevent all-out war, and as a result, he was determined to understand why St Cecil would pass along such a tale. Audley assigned a staffer to investigate."

"Where is this staffer?" the Duke asked.

Rex glanced at Dora, unsure of what to say. Although Dora had assured him they could be honest, they hadn't expected this question to arise.

Dora didn't miss a beat. "Audley was planning to pull him off the search because he feared the man was close to blowing his cover. That's when Rex and I stepped in to help. Mostly Rex, I should say. Unfortunately, we were too late. Whoever is behind this got to the agent first."

"So... that's two men missing?" Dora's father asked.

"I wish that were the case. We ventured to his flat for a meeting. There, we found him dead. Murdered," Dora added. "This is why we've been so careful with our approach to the investigation. Whoever is behind this will go to incredible lengths to keep their secret. Rex was working his way around to the key players, but the coalition fell apart before we could figure out why St Cecil did what he did."

The duke speared Dora with a stony glare while mulling over her words. "Murder and kidnapping... Those are very serious charges on their own. If Audley is right about there being an even bigger manoeuvre in progress, then I'm glad you brought me in. Is that why you took a sudden interest in politics, Rex?"

"Indeed, and I must say that it has been an eye-opening experience."

"Most of the time, it's rather dull, my boy," said the duke. "You've experienced a trial by fire."

"In more ways than one," Dora added. "The fact remains, however, that someone is up to shenanigans. Until two days ago, Rex and I had narrowed our investigation around the Liberals.

But when the government collapsed and Audley went missing, we had to take a step back. To use one of your favourite phrases, cui bono?"

"Who is going to be the end beneficiary of this situation? Why, we Tories are!" he cried with great satisfaction. "And it is about time we stopped kowtowing to Lloyd George. Setting aside our disagreements made sense in the immediate aftermath of the Great War, but that time is long past. My doubts about the man had been growing, and this nonsense with Turkey was the proverbial nail in the coffin for me and many others."

Dora and Rex exchanged glances. It was exactly as they'd thought. Rex, however, still had some questions.

"Your grace, might I ask how you first reacted to the Russian rumour? Lords Sutherland and Godfrey argue over the validity of the future risk, but what was everyone's response to word of an imminent challenge?"

"Initially, everyone was taken aback. Or, I should say, almost everyone. Audley denounced it as utter poppycock, but the others reacted more slowly. As much as it pains me to admit, I was inclined to follow Audley's lead, but only because I have some awareness of the strength of his whisper network." The duke inclined his head in Dora's direction.

Dora rewarded him with a smile. "What of your fellow Tories, Lords Sutherland and Godfrey?"

"When we originally read Mustafa Kemal's interview in the Daily Mail, eyebrows rose all over town. Sutherland demanded we support the Greeks, and so he initially agreed with Lloyd George. It didn't take long for us to recognise the way the wind blew amongst our allies. St Cecil then shared the rumour regarding the Soviets. Lloyd George waved it in the air as though it were an ace pulled from his sleeve. Sutherland and Godfrey kept quiet until the other government agencies declared the rumour to be false. After that, they didn't hold back in their criticism."

"Wait a minute," Rex interjected. "When I spoke with Lord Godfrey on my first visit to Westminster, he referred to the war supporters as bloodthirsty. That certainly didn't leave me with the impression he'd ever wanted to go to battle."

"First rule of politics, Lord Rex, is to make the most of any advantage. The press was more than happy to paint Lloyd George and the like as warmongers. Why shouldn't the Tories milk that for what it's worth?" The duke chortled to himself. "You have a lot to learn, young man. Perhaps I will take you under my auspices and teach you the political pathways."

"I'm afraid my claim on Lord Rex's free time precedes yours, Father," Dora countered. "If you don't mind, I'd like to keep the conversation on topic, at least until Lord Audley is safe at home. Now, I enjoy reading the political section of the papers well more than the average person, but over the last few months, I've had other responsibilities to occupy me. That's where we've gone wrong."

Rex struggled to make sense of Dora's comment, both because she had admitted to a shortcoming and because he had no idea where she wanted the conversation to go. "What do you mean? You've known as much about this Turkish matter as anyone else with whom I've spoken."

Dora waved off his compliment. "We've been looking at this as an isolated incident, but what if it is the final play in a long game?"

"Are you suggesting there is some sort of conspiracy going on?" Dora's father shook his head. "You've spent too much time with Audley."

"I learned this concept from you, Father. You filled your bookshelves with biographies of great rulers, and it was from reading them I grasped the idea of the long game. How many times did you tell us to think three steps ahead, or to make a short-term sacrifice if it meant winning in the end?" Dora's earnest expression underscored her plaintive words. "If the Tories are the ultimate beneficiaries of this political game, who amongst them will gain the most glory?"

The Duke of Dorset rocked back in his seat and covered his mouth with his hand. Rex saw that Dora's question had the intended effect of forcing her father to consider the unthinkable. He wouldn't want to be in his shoes.

Dora didn't let up with her barrage of questions. "Assuming the Tories carry the election, who will become Prime Minister?"

The Duke scoffed at this suggestion. "With so little time to mount a campaign, the party is not taking any chances on an unknown. I'd put my money on them selecting Bonar Law to lead again. And before you say anything, I'll tell you both that the man is seriously unwell. He'll be little more than a figurehead while the other candidates jostle for support among the ranks."

Dora crossed her arms and grimaced. "Bonar Law is the last man I'd suspect. He's always shown a propensity for doing what is best for the nation, including standing aside when Lloyd George became Prime Minister. If he is stepping into the role now, he won't leave until he is sure the government is on safe ground. We need someone who is due to gain in the immediate future. What about cabinet positions? Leader of the House of Lords?"

"Perhaps..." the duke said, although he was unconvinced.

Rex reviewed the conversations he'd overheard during his lunch with the Tory lords, and the later debate at Fitz's party. He'd assumed that Lord Sutherland and Lord Godfrey had squared off against one another for the fun of the discussion. But what if there was more to it?

"Who would be on the short list for leadership? I assume

yourself, but am I correct in thinking Sutherland and Godfrey would also enter consideration?"

Dora's father shifted his attention to Rex before answering his question. "I have little desire to take on the burden of such a role. Sutherland and Godfrey can fight it out amongst themselves. I fear for Godfrey, however. If the new PM passes Sutherland over, he'll make life miserable for whomever lands the position."

"Does Lord Godfrey know this?" Rex asked.

"He would have to be both blind and deaf to ignore Sutherland's ambition, but Godfrey won't go down without a fight." The older man shrugged his broad shoulders. "A decade ago, I'd have thrown my name into the hat and taken them both down. But now, my focus is on my family."

Dora leaned forward, reaching out with her hand so she could intertwine her fingers with those of her father. "I'm sorry, Father. You had your sights on a leadership role when I was younger. I'm sure my decision to stray so far from the nest, on top of the loss of Wills at the Somme, pulled the proverbial wind from your sails."

Her father gave her a rueful smile. "Haven't you figured it out yet, daughter of mine? Raising you and your brothers caused me so much stress over the years. Particularly you, given your propensity to thumb your nose at a traditional life. Despite the grey in my hair, the sleepless nights, and the gnawing worry in my stomach, I would not trade you children for anyone else. I am proud of you — all three of you. You don't hold me back. You inspire me to aim higher. That's why I'm choosing to step out of the limelight. It is time for you and Benedict to get the glory."

"Oh Father!" Dora cried. She squeezed his hand so tight that her fingers were white.

Even Rex found himself dashing a wayward tear from the

corner of his eye. The Duke gave a manly cough to hide his emotion and blustered until Dora eased back in her seat.

Rex fetched the bottle of Port from the sideboard and refilled the glasses, giving Dora and her father a moment to regain their composure.

When Rex returned to his seat, he resumed their earlier discussions. "From what you've said, we cannot cross either Sutherland or Godfrey from our list of potential suspects. Both men have both the wherewithal and a plausible motive for acting as an invisible hand in these current events. How can we narrow our list to one?"

"Only one surefire way I know," Dora replied. "We have to apply pressure and hope one of them will make a mistake and reveal their hand."

Rex did not know how to do that, although he was very much in favour of the idea. Thus far, all the pressure sat on his and Dora's shoulders. It would be nice to see someone else take on that burden.

The duke delivered an answer. "With that, I believe I can be of aid. There is a party meeting tomorrow to discuss how and where the Peers will show their support. Rex, why don't you accompany me?"

Rex yearned to say yes, but had a concern. "Will I be welcome?"

"If you come along with me, you will. The party is keen to gather all the support it can at this critical time. That said, it would certainly be within your prerogative to raise questions or concerns that are holding you back from a solid commitment."

Dora tilted her head to the side, giving her father a sideways look. "That's mighty devious of you, Father. You must stick close to Rex, however. Getting their backs up is an ingenious suggestion, but we must prepare for the eventuality that they'll show their hands by lashing out."

The duke gave a nod of confirmation. "I'll bring Benedict, as well. One of us will remain by Rex's side the entire time."

Rex's mouth went dry as he watched the pair plot his moves. He finally understood that when it came to the Cavendish family, the apples didn't fall far from the tree. He didn't know whom he admired more — his devious mentor, her father, or Lord Audley, who held his own against both.

Moreover, throughout the entirety of their scheming, neither Dora nor the Duke professed any doubts about his abilities.

That thought lingered in Rex's mind until the wee hours of the night. For the first time, he set aside his worries and reservations. Instead, he pictured Dora standing before him, poking her finger into his chest.

"Occam's Razor," said the imaginary Dora as she flashed him a knowing grin. "The simplest explanation is usually the right one. Everyone you admire thinks you're good enough. Instead of finding arguments against the matter, try considering we might be right."

Chapter 20
Dora doubles back

Dora studied her reflection in her dressing room mirror. The evening had gone far better than she'd dared to dream. Her parents still loved her. Benedict was in a snit, and Rex had a pathway for progressing their investigation.

And yet, she'd tossed and turned throughout the night. Why did she still have a niggling concern scratching at the back of her mind?

She had overlooked something.

Despite her arguments to the contrary, Dora was not perfect. She made mistakes, just like every other person in the world. She tried her hardest to temper her worst instincts, but those efforts worked best when she had the leisure of time.

Over the past week, she'd done little else but run from one potential clue to the next. Along the way, she'd missed something. Her subconscious knew it, but frustratingly, it failed to provide an answer.

Fortunately, she knew exactly where to turn for help.

Dora grabbed her Chinese silk dressing gown from the hanger and pulled it over her gossamer nightgown. After cinching the belt around her narrow waist, she marched down the hall and rapped on another bedroom door.

Inga answered within seconds. She wore only an old-fashioned nightgown and had a giant cowlick in the middle of her head. Her brow furrowed as she took in Dora's expression. "We've missed something, haven't we?"

"You sense it, too?" Dora asked. Her relief was immediate. "Comb your hair, put on a dressing gown, and then meet me downstairs. I'll make a pot of coffee and bring it to the dining room."

Dora could have asked Cook or Cynthia to prepare the coffee, but she brushed aside their offers. The simple tasks of pouring water and spooning coffee grounds kept Dora's hands busy and her mind free to roam. She worked backwards through her memories, remembering every word of her conversation with her father. Was that where she'd made her mistake?

Or had it been earlier... when Clark came to lunch, or while they were sneaking around Westminster? Dora tried each possibility on for size, but none of them felt right.

She carried the tray upstairs and found both Inga and Harris waiting for her in the corridor. They claimed seats on one side of the table while she prepared their cups according to their individual preferences. Inga took her coffee black like her heart, but with a single cube of sugar to sweeten her day. Harris preferred his with a heavy dose of cream. Dora was somewhere in the middle.

Silence hung over the trio. Dora wrapped her hands around her heavy ceramic mug, letting the heat warm her fingertips. Stacks of papers and files once again covered the table. Dora practically knew them by heart at this point. The handwritten notes spoke to the monotony of daily parliamentary life — endless discussions and debates, with little to show in the end. On the other side, lines and lines of legal text, made ever more lengthy due to the formality of the wording, filled the typed pages.

Dora forced her gaze upward. The answer didn't lie on the tabletop. So, what was missing?

Dora needed to mentally retrace her steps, starting this time from the beginning. It had all started with that conversation with Lord Audley.

"Help me sketch a timeline, will you?" Dora asked while handing Inga a notepad and pen. "Lord Audley assigns Murdoch to investigate St Cecil. Murdoch does as asked, including breaking into offices in Westminster. He nearly gets caught. That's enough for Audley to pull Murdoch off the task and find someone else instead. Did I miss anything?"

Inga and Harris shook their heads in unison.

"I show up and offer Rex on a silver platter. Audley accepts and instructs Murdoch to hand over his findings to date. We go to his flat. Murdoch fails to answer the door. When we get inside, the place is trashed and Murdoch is dead."

Harris jumped in, picking up the narrative. "I took control of the scene. You and Rex gathered his papers and left. You sent Archie and Basil over to help me. We tidied up everything, paid up the rent, and replaced the lock on the door before we left. We delivered Murdoch's body to Lord Audley. Then we came back home, where we found the two of you."

"Where we were busy searching through the papers," Inga added, finishing up her notes.

Dora scrunched her nose. They were getting closer, but she couldn't put her finger on what was bothering her. She held out her hand and motioned for Inga to pass her the notepad. As soon as her fingers closed on the thick cover, her subconscious sounded the alarm.

"Where are Murdoch's personal insights into the situation?" Dora scanned the table from end to end. "We've got meeting notes and documents, but nothing here tells us what was going on inside his head."

Inga's skepticism was written across her face. "What makes you think he wrote it down?"

Dora threw her hands wide. "Because that's what I would do if I had to pass an investigation to someone else! He would have documented his investigation, suspicions, theories to explore, and anything else relevant. So I ask again, where are his notes?"

Harris and Inga shrugged their shoulders.

"The killer stole them?" Harris ventured.

"If that were the case, then why kidnap Lord Audley? We've got Audley's papers. If he had them, we'd have found them. So where are they?" Dora's excitement sent her voice up a notch. "They have to be in Murdoch's flat. Rex and I took what we saw lying around. No one who works for Audley would be so careless as to leave intelligence in plain sight. Nor would they make it easy to find."

"Don't say it—" Inga cautioned.

Dora ignored the warning. "We have to go back. Right now. No one knows the man is dead. We can pretend we're visiting."

Inga's hands flew up to pull her hair. "It's barely dawn. That's far too early for any acceptable women to pay a call to a men's boarding house. Let's go later this morning, after everyone has left for work."

"The early hour is our friend! Plus, it's overcast. No one will see me if I dress in grey. I can bring Archie and Basil with me. If we can get access to the rear courtyard, it should be easy enough to use the window ledges to climb to his floor."

Inga pulled her hands free of her hair and crossed her arms. "You haven't assessed the scene. What if the windows are locked or painted shut? We — as in you and I — will go in the full daylight. Like normal people."

Dora raised her voice to continue the argument, but stopped when Harris flapped his hands.

"There's no need to scale the wall like a cat burglar. I've got Murdoch's keys!" He sat back and waited for the women to flower him with their thanks. Instead, he got smacked on the arm.

"You couldn't save that piece of information until lunchtime?" Inga snapped, glaring at her partner. "Now Dora's going to make us dress up like men and pretend we're coming back after a night-shift."

Harris blanched as her words hit home. "Oops?" He shrugged his shoulders. "There's no need for you to come along," he reminded her.

Inga's fierce growl had Harris scrambling out of her reach. He launched out of his chair and aimed for the door. "I'd better excuse myself, then. I'll ask Cook to prepare bacon baps we can eat on the way. I'll wait for you two by the car."

Inga's grumbles provided Dora with no end of entertainment while the two got dressed. Dora never minded donning a suit and waistcoat. She suspected Inga secretly enjoyed the freedom that trousers and a flat cap offered, although she'd never admit it. As Harris had pointed out, if she truly hated going undercover that much, Inga always had the option of remaining home. When the risk of real danger was high, Inga did just that. But in instances such as this, where there was little chance of discovery, Inga's resentment over being left out outweighed her preference for skirts and cardigans.

"You make a fine-looking man," Dora quipped while smoothing Inga's fake moustache into place. "You'll make an excellent husband to some nice young woman."

Inga turned her brown-eyed gaze to the skies as though she were praying for help from above.

"If your eyes roll any harder, they may end up stuck in the back of your head," Dora warned her friend. Inga's response was a blistering torrent of words not fit to print. As far as Dora was concerned, that only made the situation funnier.

Somehow, they made it to Murdoch's rented housing in one piece. The trio adopted world-weary poses, with their shoulders slumped and eyes fixed on the ground whenever someone passed nearby. They walked slowly, trudging along the hallway until they reached Murdoch's doorway.

Harris produced the key and twisted it in the lock. The door swung open, sending a cloud of musty air roiling through the door. The edge of rot had both women wrinkling their noses.

"Forget to check for stale food, did you?" Inga asked Harris after they were safely inside. Harris flushed, not needing to answer. The smell spoke for itself. He hurried over to open the windows a crack.

"Let's not extend our visit any longer than necessary," Dora said, to prevent the other two from bickering. "Put your spy caps on and search the place for potential hiding spots. We'll work one room at a time."

The kitchenette provided no space for hidden objects, with its single cupboard, cook plate, and chipped sink. They moved into the sitting area. It took all three of them working together to lift the furniture and check behind and underneath each piece.

The only thing they found were dust bunnies and a moulding fish and chips wrapper.

"Aha!" Harris shouted in satisfaction when he spotted the dark green-stained paper. "See, it wasn't me!"

"Yes, dear. I'm sure that spoiled half-pint of milk I found had nothing to do with the odour," Inga remarked while giving him a side-eyed glance.

Their steady patter helped Dora to hold her nerves at bay. There had to be something hidden here for them to find. The longer it took to locate Murdoch's notes, the more Dora's stomach roiled. The pithy banter kept her in the here and now, instead of the must-be and what ifs.

"Nothing for it," Harris groaned. "We'll have to check the bedroom. If Murdoch's spirit is lingering there, I can only hope it decides to be of assistance."

"If he's held here by unfinished business, I'd say we have an excellent chance of getting a nudge in the right direction. Let's go." Dora marched into the bedroom and stood in the middle of the room, waiting for an icy touch to guide her.

When nothing happened, Inga snapped her fingers to get Dora's attention. "Before you call in a medium, might I suggest we try this the old-fashioned way and actually search?"

Dora dropped her shoulders like a scolded school girl and groaned, "If we have to, Mum... No wait, make that, Father. No mother of mine is going to have a moustache."

Harris snickered until Inga glared him into silence.

They stayed silent while sliding their hands under the mattress and behind the wooden headboard. Inga pulled out the drawers from the nightstand and then felt all around inside the cavities.

Dora sent Harris into the bathroom while she took on the wardrobe. On the positive side, it was tall and narrow, with drawers and a mirror on the right side and hanging storage on the left. Dora dragged a chair in from the other room and climbed onto the seat. She checked on top of and behind the large mirror. She moved the chair around and reached up to search the flat top of the storage area.

The drawers were tidier than she expected. One held shirts, another socks and men's shorts. The bottom drawer contained two sets of nightshirts. A paper edge caught her eye and sent her hopes soaring. It turned out to be a set of racy French postcards rather than a journal.

Dora tucked the postcards into her trousers pocket.

"Find something?" Inga asked.

"Yes, but it will be of more interest to Archie and Basil than to us." Dora pulled a card free and held it up for Inga to see. Inga's snort of laughter had Harris asking whether they were all right.

The only place left to check was the wardrobe storage space. Dora knew Murdoch's body wasn't in there any longer. But that didn't stop her from feeling squeamish about opening the wooden door.

She counted to three and pulled the door open in a rush.

The cupboard was empty, just as it was supposed to be.

Not entirely empty... Two shirts and three pairs of black trousers hung from wooden hangers. They'd been shoved to the side to make space for the killer to stash the body. Dora suspected there'd originally been three shirts, but Harris had removed a bloodstained one when he'd cleared the scene.

He hadn't been able to do anything about the dark red stain that marked the bottom. It was dry, but the thin wood had warped due to the moisture.

Dora stared at the stain, seeing not the mark but the man who'd bled there. It required no great mental gymnastics to identify the similarities between herself and Murdoch. Both spies, both gambling with their life, and reporting into the same man.

It was enough to make Dora's blood run cold.

The murmur of voices pulled her from her reverie. Unlike her, Murdoch didn't have anyone to watch his back. She made a silent vow to properly show her thanks to Harris and Inga once this was done.

She stepped backwards and eased the door closed, but a shadow in the far corner caught her eye. She pulled the storage door open again and shifted until the light of the room illuminated the area in question.

Where the corner edge should have been, there was a narrow gap, barely larger than an inch. Just wide enough to allow a small tool... or a woman's finger to fit inside.

"Over here," Dora called to her friends. She lowered onto her knees and reached her hand into the cabinet, taking care to avoid the blackening stain. It took two tugs to get the false bottom of the cupboard to come free.

Dora wasted no time. She grabbed the cloth-wrapped packet from its hiding spot and passed it to Harris. "Stuff this inside your coat. We'll look at it when we're home."

Chapter 21
A visit to Carlton House

The sun failed to break through the thick clouds covering the sky. Rex had happily turned over driving responsibilities to his grandmother's chauffeur, wanting to use the ride to organise his thoughts. However, when he arrived at the Duke of Dorset's home, he was no closer to having a plan of attack than when he left.

It was as though the clouds in the sky had seeped into his head, clogging his mind and turning everything into pea soup. Nothing in his training with Dora had prepared Rex for this moment. His newfound skills for picking locks and climbing roofs were of no use here. Was he supposed to go on the attack?

He asked himself what Dora would do in his shoes. He didn't have to ponder overlong.

Dora said over and over again that power came from knowledge. Therefore, he should use his time with the duke wisely, to learn as much as he could about their potential foes.

The butler answered the door and invited Rex inside. After passing off his coat and hat, Rex ventured into the drawing room. Dora's mother, the Duchess of Dorset, sat waiting on the sofa. Her eyes reminded him of the seaside on a summer's day, so unlike Dora's brilliant green.

Yet, the similarities between the pair were impossible to ignore. The classic lines of her simple day dress highlighted her slender figure and erect posture. She had the same habit as Dora of enjoying her periodicals with her morning cup of tea. Even the lipstick staining the edge of her teacup reminded Rex of Dora.

The duchess closed a magazine she'd been reading and set it beside her on the sofa, giving Rex her undivided attention. Her gaze missed nothing, but was soft enough to put Rex at ease. "Good morning, Lord Rex. My husband is finishing some work in his study and Benedict is yet to make an appearance downstairs. I hope you don't mind, but I thought to keep you company."

"Not at all," Rex replied. He chose to sit opposite from her, on a wingback chair with an elaborately embroidered cushion. "If anything, I'm sorry to have disturbed you so early in the morning."

"I'm an early riser. Always have been. I woke even earlier this morning, as my head was too full of questions about my daughter to allow me to sleep. In many ways, she doesn't appear to have changed at all, and yet, she is, at the same time, a stranger to me. I can't help but envy you for the time you've had together."

Rex's smile wobbled, and he shifted in his chair. "We're not, err, that is to say..." He stopped talking to give his mind time to catch up with his mouth. There was no way to say it but to blurt it out. "We're colleagues. That's all."

"I see..." the duchess's voice trailed off, but the quirk of her lips left the opposite impression of what her words said.

"She is my mentor," Rex hurried to add. "If I someday master half of what she knows, I'll count myself a lucky man."

The duchess's smile widened as she tilted her head to the side, her gaze sharpening. "You admire her. I didn't expect that."

"Of course I admire her!" Rex blurted, feeling his ire rise at whatever she was insinuating.

Dora's mother waved her hand to restore the calm. "As a child, Dora evoked many an emotion from those around her — anger, jealousy, annoyance, and consternation come to mind. The other night, I saw the way the people at the ball looked at her now that she is an adult. Much was the same, but for the men, lust sits atop the list. When I watched you two interact last night, I saw something different. From both of you. I don't think you fully realise just how lucky a man you are, Lord Rex."

Rex had no response to offer. If he understood what she was saying... No. No, that was too much to even contemplate. Besides, the woman barely knew her adult child. Dora flirted with everyone. He was not special in that regard, no matter what Lady Cavendish believed.

The arrival of Lord Benedict and Lord Cavendish saved Rex from coming up with any words. The duchess kissed her husband on the cheek and bid him goodbye, leaving the room with a trace of perfume and a lipstick-stained teacup as the only proof of her earlier presence.

Benedict scrunched his brow and studied Rex. "Is everything okay, old chap?"

"Of course," Rex replied, telling himself as much as Benedict. "We should be on our way."

Out front, a Rolls-Royce Silver Ghost saloon car waited to carry the men to the Carlton Club. The infamous seat of the Conservative Party, it would play host to today's discussions of future leadership positions and party platform. Benedict claimed the front position next to the family driver, leaving Rex to join the duke in the rear.

The duke sprawled across the bench, with one arm resting

on the car door and the other along the top of the seat. He wore all the trappings expected of a titled man, but yet exuded the fierce energy of an animal preparing to hunt. Dora's father was relishing the challenge before him. Never mind that these men were his peers, and in some cases, friends. That wouldn't slow him from poking and prodding them into a reaction.

So that was where Dora got her courage to antagonise Lord Audley!

"You seem in fine form today, Father," Benedict said, turning sideways so he could see the rear of the car.

"I'm not ashamed to agree, son. Your mother has had me away in the countryside for so long that I'd nearly forgotten how much I enjoy matching wits against my peers." He chuckled darkly. "Let's hope they've forgotten as well."

Benedict grimaced and twisted back to face the front. "Don't tell me you're reconsidering your decision to leave London, Father."

The duke didn't answer, instead choosing to wink at Rex while Benedict wasn't looking.

Rex didn't envy Benedict's position. As far as he could tell, the man had enjoyed the delights of living on his own for the past two years. Worse yet, his mother might take an interest in seeing him finally married off. As the only male in the line, he had his duties.

For once, Rex was delighted to be the second son.

But Benedict was certainly going to be furious... and he'd likely take out his frustration on Dora and Rex.

There was nothing Rex could do about that now. He turned his mind back to the challenge at hand. He had a question for the duke.

"Before we arrive, do you have any advice regarding Godfrey and Sutherland?"

"After sleeping on it, in my opinion, it's best if we divide and conquer. I'll needle Lord Godfrey. For Sutherland, you're best placed to go after the man. You must highlight his main deficiency."

"What's that?"

"He's never fought in a war. Point that out at an opportune moment and you'll cost him the respect of the younger generations."

Rex nodded his understanding and mulled over the suggestion. Having spent time at the war front as a courier and fighter, and interacted with many in the senior levels of the military, Rex's battlefield bravery wasn't in doubt. That said, he'd never been one to look down upon someone else because they hadn't served. Plenty of men stayed close to the home front for perfectly valid reasons.

They arrived at the club before Rex had time to inquire how Lord Sutherland had spent his time. He had to assume whatever explanation there was; it wasn't going to trip Rex up. Dora trusted her father to help them. Therefore, Rex had to trust the duke as well.

Once inside, the Carlton Club was humming with an energy unusual to such a staid institution. A palpable sense of urgency and excitement hung in the air. The Tories knew this was their time to shine. They'd done the impossible, banding together to topple the government and force an election.

Fortunes would be made over the coming days as MPs and Peers jockeyed for positions of power within the new government. Some would become ministers, others backbench vocalists. Opportunities to make a name for oneself existed in both places.

The duke ensured they arrived in time for a Peers debate over the House of Lords position on key pieces of the Tory platform. The new PM would expect the Lords' blind support on whatever he set forth. As peers for life, the Lords would fall in line when they wanted, and not at anyone's demand.

The men in suits filed into one of the club's larger meeting rooms. The duke left Rex with Benedict and took a seat on the raised dais beside the other senior peers. Lord Godfrey sat heavily on his wooden chair and studied the crowd over the top of his pince-nez.

Lord Sutherland claimed the centre seat, looking to all the world like a king on his throne. His thick white hair enhanced his reputation as a distinguished member of the party. The ruddy colour in his cheeks spoke of good health as much as fine wine.

A footman rang a bell to call the room to order, and the discussion began.

Rex and Benedict sat in the middle of the room, in the second row of chairs. Rex had time to take in the decor while Lord Godfrey began his introduction. Yellow fabric covered the walls, making the space seem much brighter than the dreary day would allow. The vibrant colour contrasted with the mahogany floors and heavy wooden chairs. If only the tone of the debate took the same cue.

The three esteemed peers wasted no time in getting into arguments with one another. Godfrey no sooner proposed a topic than Sutherland disagreed. The Duke of Dorset sat back for the most part, popping up now and again with a zinger of his own. They discussed the economy, foreign affairs, women's rights, and the other major issues of the day. Despite seemingly being on the same side, behind these closed doors, they were free to highlight their differences. This was most easily done by telling the other men they were wrong, in no uncertain terms.

The audience was hardly quiet. Despite the layout of the room, in theory, the men inside were all equals. The elder statesmen had an undeniable gravitas, but that didn't make them immune to challenges from the floor. Even Benedict, one of the newer lords in the house, spoke up from time to time.

Rex remained silent. He played his role of fly on the wall to the hilt, clocking every twist and turn of the debate. He noticed the subtle differences between what Lords Godfrey and Sutherland said versus what their body language and facial expressions communicated.

In this, Dora's training served him well. To all the world, Rex escorted Dora around town. None knew how much he learned with every outing. During visits to parks, the opera, and restaurants, she'd challenged Rex to imagine the conversations taking place around them.

Lord Godfrey put up a good front, but the slump of his shoulders gave Rex the impression he was resigned to playing second fiddle. He held his own each time the duke baited him with a remark. But when Lord Sutherland took him to task, he backed down after two rounds of debate.

Try as he might, Rex couldn't get the image of Lord Godfrey as a power-hungry killer to make sense.

Thus, he turned his full focus on Lord Sutherland. In doing so, he finally listened closely to what the man was saying.

Lord Sutherland stood up and paced along the front of the dais, waving his hands while he made his point. "The days of the Liberal and Labour parties dictating our decisions are over! Together, we will take our battle for control of the Commons to the doorsteps. We'll raise our banners high and assert our right to lead. There will be no enemies left behind. By the time this is over, every heart in this country will bleed Tory blue!"

On and on he went, using battle metaphors. At first, Rex thought the man didn't understand the impact of his words. As the duke had said, Lord Sutherland never experienced the true terror of the enemy breathing down the back of his neck.

Rex chanced a look at the men on either side of him.

Benedict wore a frown. Lord Fitz, Rex's old school chum, seemed similarly ill at ease. The older generation, however, nodded their agreement. Men with white hair pounded their wooden canes against the floor to show their enthusiasm. The hardship of war had long since faded from their memory, and only the recollections of their glory days remained.

Rex's gut churned. He knew what they expected of him. He wasn't supposed to call attention to himself by making a speech in this room where he was little more than a guest. His only assignment was to needle Lord Sutherland with a few well-placed barbs.

But there was no way Rex would leave with such a call to arms still hanging in the air. Fury prevailed over common sense, driving him to his feet when he should have raised his hand and asked permission to speak.

"I beg to differ, Lord Sutherland," he said in a ringing tone. "My brothers and I did not bleed on foreign soil, only to come home and view one another as the new enemy. Men who valued collaboration over being contrarian rebuilt our country these past five years. The extension of voting rights to all men only underscores the importance of building a coalition, rather than tearing one another down. How dare you incite us to war! A truly intelligent man would fight tooth and nail to retain peace."

When Rex paused to catch his breath, he felt the weight of so many stares crash into his shoulders. He found himself on his feet. He didn't even remember standing up. Now head and shoulders above everyone else, Rex realised that every man in the room was looking his way. He wasn't even a member of the Tory party, nor did he sit in the House of Lords. And yet, there he stood, declaring his opinion in front of God and man.

No one needed to speak the words aloud. Rex had overstepped the bounds of propriety when he dared to take a party elder to task.

His gaze slid past the duke's stunned expression, hardly noting it. Lord Sutherland's face was flushed with anger. But it was Lord Godfrey who gave Rex pause. The man was aghast at Rex's social gaff.

The roiling frustration that had sustained his lengthy speech drained from Rex's body, leaving behind the sour taste of embarrassment. Now that he'd attracted the attention of everyone in the room, there was no possibility of achieving his mission. All he could do was tuck tail and make a hasty retreat.

Rex fled.

Chapter 22
The ten-pound bet

To the casual observer, Dora and Inga appeared to be going about their normal activities. Seated in the drawing room, they flipped through the day's periodicals, each with a cup of tea in hand.

In truth, it took all their self-control to keep from leaping to their feet and running off to save the day. Dora was confident she knew who had kidnapped Lord Audley, and more importantly, why. Despite that knowledge, she was sitting tight.

After returning home from their search of Murdoch's flat and realising what they'd found, the women changed back into normal clothing. They sat down for lunch, adjourned to the drawing room, read the papers, and exchanged polite conversation. If they shifted in their seats more often, no one made a comment. Dora and Inga were in firm agreement — this was Rex's mission. It would be wrong to leave him out of the ending.

As often was the case, doing what was right wasn't easy. Inga reached the limit of her patience first. She set her empty cup on its saucer with a clatter and tossed her magazine aside. "What is taking them so long?"

Dora raised her eyebrows. "A room full of men discussing their plans for dominating the country, and potentially the world? My word, we'll be lucky if Rex and my father make it back by nightfall."

Inga laughed, but soon enough, they saw Dora was wrong.

Not long after, the front door swung open and Rex came rushing inside. He didn't bother with any of the social niceties, such as ringing the buzzer, waiting to be invited in, or removing his cap. Rex walked into the drawing room with his face deathly pale, opened his mouth and closed it just as quick. He shook his head, and then spun around and left the way he came.

Dora leapt to her feet and followed behind. Rex turned away from the front door and strode deeper into the house, not stopping until he reached the library. He fumbled around with the bookshelf until Dora understood his intention. She rested her hand on his arm to stall his movements and then reached past him to release the catch on the door to her secret room.

He roused himself enough to give her a grateful smile and then stumbled the last few steps until he fell into a chair. Once seated, he folded over and buried his face in his hands.

Dora needed no primer to understand what was bothering him. She recognised the signs, writ large in his every movement. He had failed in his task.

She perched on the armrest of his chair and leaned her body against his, wrapping an arm around his shoulders. "Want to talk about it?"

"Not yet," he mumbled, his words almost incomprehensible from behind his hands.

Dora pursed her lips and pondered her next move. "Do you want to be alone? Or would good news help distract you from self-flagellating?"

Rex lowered his hands and tilted his head so he could meet her gaze. "News? From Lord Audley?"

Dora slid her arm free and shifted until she sat on the chair across from him. "Close. We returned to Murdoch's flat this morning and searched it properly. We found his investigation notes and photographs he took of sensitive papers. I finally understand how the pieces of this puzzle fit together and where we'll find Lord Audley."

Rex blinked his eyes against the rapid onslaught of information. "You know where Lord Audley is? Then why are you sitting here with me?"

Dora cupped his face in her palm. "I waited for you. You said you wanted us to do this together, and so we shall. Tell me when you are ready to go."

She didn't need to ask twice. Rex jumped up and felt for his cap and coat, blushing when he discovered he was still wearing both. The noise of their hurried movements attracted Inga's attention. She met them in the library doorway with Dora's coat, scarf, and hat in hand.

"Make sure you deliver this to Audley when you see him," she instructed in a no-nonsense tone while passing Dora a plain white envelope.

Dora performed a precise salute and led Rex out to her car. Harris already had the engine running. Within fifteen minutes, he pulled over in front of a large Mayfair home not far from where Rex lived.

"Here?" Rex asked, taking in the sharp lines of the Georgian facade. "Whose home is this?"

Dora crooked her finger, beckoning him to follow. She rapped the heavy brass knocker with a steady hand.

A middle-aged man answered, wearing the black suit of an upper class butler. He stared down the length of his nose at the unexpected guests waiting at the threshold. "May I help you?"

"We're here to visit Lord St Cecil," Dora announced in a

firm tone. "Rex, be a dear and pass the man your card so he can announce us."

Rex's eyes were wide in confusion, but he did as instructed. His name worked better than any key at opening the door. After a brief moment to ask whether St Cecil would see them, the butler showed Dora and Rex inside.

A footman took their coats and hats, and then the butler escorted them along a marble-tiled hall until they arrived at a game room in the rear of the house. Two heavily muscled men guarded the door. They glared menacingly at Dora and Rex before finally moving aside.

Dora spared no time to examine the leather-upholstered furniture, nor the book-lined shelves covering one wall. Her full attention landed on the men sitting near the fireplace. Rex choked at the sight and Dora elbowed him to keep him from revealing their hand.

Not that he could. Nothing she'd said on the way had prepared him to find Lord St Cecil and Lord Audley sitting together like two old school mates reminiscing about the good old days.

"Ah, Lord Rex, how nice to see you. I wondered when you'd make your way over. And you've brought Miss Laurent along with you." Audley pulled his watch from his pocket and checked the time. "A full day early. St Cecil, you owe me a ten-pound note and a full explanation."

Lord St Cecil was too gobsmacked to reply. Rex was equally stunned into silence. Dora stepped into the breach to keep Rex from saying something revealing.

Playing her role of society darling, she clapped her hands in delight and exclaimed, "Rexy-darling, how clever were you to figure out where Lord Audley was hiding? Here I thought we were simply playing the role of mail carrier. Do you still want me to give this envelope to Lord St Cecil?" Dora waved the envelope in question in the air.

Dora had to give it to Rex. He was quick on the uptake. He turned to look at her and caught the glance she flicked in Lord Audley's direction.

"I found it in Lord Audley's study, so I believe we should pass it along to him first. We'll let him decide what to do with it next." Rex took the envelope from Dora and opened it, acting as though he were double-checking that the contents were unchanged. It was the right size to hold an A4 letter, but inside was a single photograph. Rex took only a second to skim it before shoving it back inside and handing it to Lord Audley.

Lord Audley extracted it with care and held it up so he could examine the contents. He sniffed in disapproval and then thrust it in St Cecil's direction. "So, this was your plan. You made Sutherland put it in writing?"

St Cecil paled and babbled nonsensically until Audley waved him to a stop.

"Lord Rex, Miss Laurent, please take a seat. Lord St Cecil owes you an explanation as much as me. Might as well make yourselves comfortable. I don't imagine this will be a short tale."

Rex availed himself of a nearby sofa and invited Dora to join him. "For starters, I'd like to know why his lordship kidnapped you off the street. I was waiting outside, just as you'd asked, but was too shocked to react in time to rescue you."

"Oh my word, there were witnesses! Who else saw?" St Cecil gasped as his face drained of colour. He leapt to his feet and hurried over to the drinks cart, where he poured himself a shot of whiskey. He tossed it back and then remembered he wasn't alone.

Rex and Audley declined his offers of a drink. Instead, the latter told him to sit down and speak up.

Lord St Cecil took a deep breath, steeling himself for what he was about to admit, and launched into the full story.

"We came up with the idea one evening, after many rounds of drinks and hands of cards. Sutherland was railing again about his political genius going overlooked. I made a flippant remark that if he was so smart, he'd come up with a way to ensure his rise to the top. I hardly expected him to take the challenge seriously."

"But he did," Audley said, waving St Cecil on.

"Aye, he did. He made me the devil of an offer. All I had to do was pass along a rumour. He assured me it would be proven false in short order, and there'd be no hint of treason. In exchange, when the Tories won the next election, Sutherland would see me appointed to a cabinet position. The photograph shows our agreement."

"This was the rumour of the Russian involvement with the Turks?" Rex clarified.

St Cecil nodded, unable to bring himself to say the words. "I thought for sure Lloyd George would dismiss it as poppycock, but he was too enthralled with the idea of going to war. I will admit that the Prime Minister's own actions dismayed me sufficiently to decide Sutherland was right. Lloyd George needed to go. But you, sir, were like a dog with a bone. You kept asking questions."

Lord Audley frowned. "That is my responsibility, St Cecil, as you know well. In my shoes, would you have turned a blind eye?"

St Cecil ignored the question. "Sutherland came to visit me in my office one evening. He assured me there was no chance anyone might cotton on to our actions. I had the only copy of our agreement, and I'd hidden it away. But as Sutherland left, we spotted another man dashing out of my outer office. I recognised him as a new staff member and promised Sutherland I'd pay the man off to keep him quiet."

"Did you?" Audley's tone was free of emotion, but he had the look of a cobra preparing to strike.

"I never saw the man again. I assumed Sutherland must have got to him before me and made some kind of offer..." St Cecil skipped his gaze between Lord Audley and Rex. "He didn't though, did he?"

Rex shook his head, causing St Cecil to blanch.

"Then what I did next was not in vain." St Cecil fixed his eyes on Audley. "I thought it was done, but soon after, you showed up at Westminster with Lord Rex at your side. I'd never heard of you acting as a mentor. It was then I realised that Murdoch was your man, and you were at it again with Lord Rex. The only way to keep you both safe was to remove you from the game. I knew you'd never go willingly, so I arranged to have my men kidnap you from the street. Surely now you understand why it wasn't safe for you to leave?"

"Don't expect me to express my gratitude," Lord Audley said with a scowl on his face. "Should the necessity to remove me from the field arise in the future, I'd encourage you to give me the chance to agree before resorting to force."

"Understood," St Cecil said and then gulped.

Lord Audley glared one last time for good measure before finally moving on with the conversation. "Now that we're all caught up, I'm keen to find out what you've learned in my absence, Lord Rex."

"The Tories are preparing for the upcoming election. Sutherland is making an obvious play for the role of leader of the House of Lords. He made some rather infuriating statements, and I'm embarrassed to admit I lost my cool. However, I'm neither a Tory nor a Peer, so my opinion counts for little."

"Forget about party loyalties. Sutherland can't take a cabinet position," St Cecil hastened to say. "He isn't fit. You have to stop him!"

Audley tsked. "I believe the word you meant to say was *we*, good man. The three of us will have to confront him."

"And the Duke of Dorset," Dora added, piping up for the first time in a while. She met Lord Audley's gaze head-on and didn't waver. "He's been remarkably helpful to Lord Rex while you were indisposed."

"Interesting..." Lord Audley studied Dora's expression closely.

She took great care to keep her features soft. Her world still stood, and she was as undaunted as ever.

"St Cecil, call for your car to come around. Lord Rex and Miss Laurent, we'll regroup at the Carlton Club. If the Tory event is running all day, I'm sure both Cavendish and Sutherland are still there."

Dora slipped her arm through Rex's and hurried him out the door, barely pausing to collect their coats on the way. She noted with satisfaction Rex's upbeat tempo and bright countenance. It was a far cry from the half-broken man who'd entered her home two hours earlier.

When he opened the car door for her, she sidled up close and said, "Cheer up, Rex. Stop worrying so much about how everything will happen."

"What do you suggest I do instead?" he asked, with a twinkle in his eye.

"The same thing I do, old chap," she said, patting him on the cheek. "If history is any guide, I'll keep on trusting it will all come out right in the end."

Chapter 23
A final confrontation

Rex was indeed relieved by this sudden turn of events. He did his level best to follow Dora's advice and quash the last of his embarrassment. Yes, he'd likely made a fool of himself in front of the Tories, but life would go on and no one was worse for the wear.

Rex didn't entirely regret what he said. If time travel were a possibility, he would not choose to go back and prevent himself from entering the Carlton Club. Sutherland spoke dangerous words without a care for anyone but himself.

Thus, when the truth came out, it came as little surprise to Rex that Sutherland had spearheaded the series of events that left Murdoch dead.

But what to do about Sutherland? Justice demanded he pay a price for his deed. In reality, a man of his standing had little chance of ending up on the chopping block.

Dora must have somehow intuited the direction of Rex's thoughts. She laid a gentle hand on his arm and squeezed. "Lord Audley will hold Sutherland to account. I promise."

Rex caught the Duke of Dorset leaving the club.

"Rex, my boy! I was on my way to find you after your abrupt

departure." The duke glanced at Dora and added, "Did you go off in search of reinforcements?"

Rex flushed. "Err, in some ways, yes. If you can spare a moment, hop into the car and I'll explain where I've been."

Rex took a long lap around the neighbouring streets while Dora explained everything to her father. The duke's expression darkened with each twist in the tale until his eyes burned with fury.

"At least Audley is safe. I'll gladly stand by his side to confront Lord Sutherland. I can't imagine a reasonable defence Sutherland might offer, but I don't put it past him to try."

This time when Rex parked outside the club, Lords Audley and St Cecil were waiting on the pavement out front. The Duke of Dorset exited the car first and made his way over to say his hellos. Rex was ready to follow, but stopped when he noticed Dora hadn't moved.

"Aren't you coming along?"

"I can't," she replied, looking none too happy. "No women allowed inside the club."

"But... they'll have to make an exception!" Rex was indignant. It wasn't right to leave Dora out, particularly not at the very end.

Dora gave a firm shake of her head. "We've called enough attention to me as it is. Theodora Laurent wouldn't force her way into a private club to confront an old man. If she went in at all, it would be for a far more scintillating reason. I'll wait here until you're done. Now hurry, the others are leaving you behind."

Rex looked toward the door to see this was indeed true. Dora flicked her wrist to hurry him on. Although he hated walking off without her, he forced his feet to move forward.

With the Duke of Dorset in their midst, the group of men had no trouble gaining access to the club. The duke led them to a small study, set aside for private conversations, and asked a footman to fetch Lord Sutherland.

The room featured ornate finishes, including a heavily carved mantle and glittering chandelier. Bookshelves lined one wall, while the other had a sideboard with decanters on display. The furniture was sparse and uncomfortable. The designers had not envisioned this room as a refuge, so much as a temporary meeting space.

While they waited, the men chose their seats with care. The intimate room offered few options. Dora's father was quick to claim one of the wingback chairs. Lords Audley and St Cecil both eyed the remaining wingback, but then thought better of it. No one wanted to be seated next to Lord Sutherland on the small sofa, in the proverbial line of fire, such as it was. In silent agreement, they opted to share the velvet upholstered sofa, sitting shoulder to shoulder.

"Rex, be a good lad and shift that chair around so we'll all be able to look Lord Sutherland in the face," Audley directed.

After Rex completed his task to everyone's satisfaction, he took up a position in the rear of the room, leaning against a half-filled bookshelf. He crossed his arms over his chest and waited for the showdown to begin.

Lord Sutherland arrived in short order. His white hair shone like snow under the sun in the bright lights of the chandelier. He had a smile pasted on his face, but it slipped when his gaze landed upon Lords St Cecil and Audley, sitting cosily on the sofa. His gait hitched, but he caught himself and straightened so quickly that Rex thought he'd imagined it.

Lord Sutherland spread his arms wide and feigned surprise. "St Cecil and Audley, I hardly expected to see the two of you here today. Or here at all, for that matter. Neither of you are party members."

Neither man responded.

Dora's father had a face of stone, his expression hard and cold of any emotion. "Take a seat, Sutherland."

"I'm afraid now isn't a good time for one of our chats, Cavendish..."

The duke gave him no quarter. His voice vibrated with barely held fury. "Sit down, I said."

Lord Sutherland sat in the wingback.

Rex held perfectly still, almost fading into the woodwork as the older lords faced off with one another. He was fortunate to be in the room at all. He didn't dare make a sound for fear of reminding them he looked on.

The Duke of Dorset gave Lord Audley a single nod, ceding the floor to his peer.

Lord Audley uncrossed his legs and sat up straight, leaning forward while speaking in a low tone. "Sutherland, we've known one another for eons by now. Until this week, I'd say we knew everything there was to know about one another. But it has come to my attention that you have a skeleton hidden in your closet, one which is of prime interest to myself and Lord Cavendish."

Sutherland chuckled. "What words you choose, Audley! I can't imagine what bald lies St Cecil has told you, but I've nothing to hide. Certainly no skeletons, as you so elegantly put it."

"What of a corpse in the cupboard?" Audley parried.

At this, Sutherland choked, causing a vicious smile to form on Lord Audley's face. It was a fearsome grin, full of threat and devoid of friendship. Rex shivered.

The game was up. Audley raised his eyebrows in a silent invitation for Sutherland to offer an explanation.

Sutherland's eyes flicked left and right. He sat quietly, weighing the pros and cons of possible defences. Rex had no idea what to expect.

He never would have predicted Sutherland's choice.

Sutherland rolled his shoulders back and sat upright. He was unbowed by the censure in the other men's gazes. "You three cast judgement upon my actions. I'm sure you think me not worth the dirt on the bottoms of your shoes. Do not expect me to roll over and bare my throat to you. As you say, we have walked many a mile together. I, too, remember where the bodies are buried. So what if mine is more literal than yours?"

"So what?" Lord Cavendish exploded, interrupting Lord Sutherland. His green eyes glowed like a demon. "The chasm between the proverbial and literal in this case is too immense to ignore! You killed a man! And for what? Power?"

Rex expected Sutherland to cower under the onslaught of words, but the duke's shouts had the opposite effect. Lord Sutherland actually laughed in Dora's father's face.

"You speak as though that word is blasphemy, when you all worship at its altar, same as I do. Which one of you will dare to hold me to account? You will pay with your secrets, same as will I. Not one of you is spotless — you cannot get to where we are by playing by the rules. Do your best, but don't be surprised if I choose not to stand still while you fire."

Rex waited for Dora's father to parry Sutherland's threat with a sharp riposte. To his horror, the man stayed silent.

Rex slid his gaze to St Cecil, the man who'd helped fuel the madman. St Cecil shifted uncomfortably in his seat and kept his gaze firmly fixed on the floor. He had no more desire than the Duke of Dorset to see his failings writ large across the papers.

But Rex still had one hope left.

Lord Audley.

Rex had never seen the man back down from a challenge, not against Dora or anyone else. Indeed, Lord Audley was already opening his mouth to reply, but Sutherland held up a hand to stop him.

"Beware of setting me in your sights, Audley. I'm sure all of Westminster will be interested in the learning about the spy you set among us. I am aware of your network of people. How well will they withstand the spotlight? Even if I can't provide their names, it is enough for me to tell the world they exist. The news hacks will turn over every stone for me. I won't have to lift a finger."

Lord Audley clenched his jaw so tight that the muscle in his cheek ticked from the effort. To give him his due, he didn't so much as cast a glance in Rex's direction. In his silence, he made it abundantly clear that he would not throw his people onto the bonfire in order to take Sutherland out.

Rex's gut churned, and a cold sweat broke out across his brow. He had the same rising urge he'd felt before, to stand against the injustice by speaking out.

But how could he do it if these powerful men had failed? He desperately wished Dora was there, standing by his side to whisper words of advice.

But she was outside in the car, oblivious to the rapidly shifting winds of justice. Lord Sutherland seemed to grow larger, his feral grin wider, and his clutch on control tighter.

There had to be someone capable of putting a stop to the madman before he hurt someone else.

The answer struck Rex like a punch in the chest.

He was that someone. If he didn't step forward, Murdoch's death would have been in vain.

What would Dora do? She'd put her hand on his back and shove him forward with all her strength. His days of meandering through life were over. It was time for him to face his challenges head-on.

"I will hold you to account," Rex declared.

Every man in the room spun at Rex's words. They'd forgotten he was there.

Rex kept his focus on Lord Sutherland. "You and I are veritable strangers. There is nothing you can use against me. Spend all the time you like spinning your wheels. I will speak out. I will not back down. After all, I spent my formative years staring across the battlefield, watching my friends and enemies get injured and die. Trust me when I say it is impossible for you, of all people, to cause me to fear."

Rex's words ripped through the group. Lord Audley, St Cecil, and Lord Cavendish gazed back at him in admiration.

Lord Sutherland struggled to remain defiant, but Rex's sharp words speared him through the chest.

"Don't make the mistake of thinking me alone, either," Rex added. "Once word gets out of your treachery, men will flock to my side. No one will stand with a traitor, not once your deeds are cast into the light."

With each word Rex said, Lord Sutherland's shoulders drooped until he crumpled in on himself. He aged before Rex's very eyes. Without the power to sustain him, he was little more than an old man.

Rex didn't need to remain for the fallout. He'd done his part.

Lord Audley agreed. "Sutherland, if you will remain quiet, I will spare you the indignity of being hauled out of here for everyone to see."

Sutherland gave a single nod. With that, all was done. Lord Cavendish thanked Rex for his dedication and sent him on his way.

As Rex left the club, his soul cried out for warmth. He knew just where to find everything he needed to feel human again. He didn't need to look any further than the gorgeous woman with hair the colour of the sun-kissed gold waiting for him in his car.

Chapter 24
A happy reunion

The Dowager Duchess of Rockingham once again agreed to play host to an impromptu supper. In truth, it had required little begging once she heard the names for the guest list: Lord and Lady Cavendish - the Duke and Duchess of Dorset, Lord Audley, her grandson Rex, and Theodora Laurent.

Prior to that evening, Lords Audley and Cavendish hadn't found themselves seated across from one another at a dinner table in years. Everyone in society knew that the two were worse than oil and water, more likely to end up demanding swords at dawn than socialising with the other guests.

But tonight, for one night only, the two had declared a truce, due to their shared interest in thanking Dora and Rex.

The dowager duchess outdid herself, serving a six-course dinner paired with the finest wines. She and Lady Cavendish kept the conversations on firm ground. Plenty of toasts were made in recognition of all they'd accomplished... not only solving a crime, but also ensuring the country remained in safe hands.

After dinner, the unlikely group adjourned to the drawing

room. Sheffield, the dowager's butler, offered glasses of Port, Madeira, and cognac to the men and women, and then left them on their own.

The dowager sat in her usual wingback, resplendent in diamonds and pearls. Dora and her mother sat together on a small sofa, seeming soft and lovely if one ignored the steel in their gazes. The men stood near the fireplace in their tails and white ties, puffing away on expensive Cuban cigars. Despite their finery, they didn't bother with the ceremony of using titles or formal address.

The dowager duchess only had eyes for her grandson. "I still can't believe it, Rex! You actually stood up to that old gasbag, Lord Sutherland?"

Rex rubbed a hand over the back of his neck and shifted uncomfortably at being put on the spot. "I wish you'd let it go, Grandmama. I wasn't supposed to speak out the way I did."

Dora watched Rex blush and, much like the dowager, felt a swell of pride. Her first proper student had passed each and every test with flying colours, including his most difficult. She took pity on him and spoke out to get his attention. "What you did was truly incredible, Rex, for two reasons. The first is you mastered the hardest part of life as a spy, and that is to follow one's gut instinct, even if it means breaking all the rules. The second reason is even more important. You spoke from your heart, even when you understood doing so might cost you everything. If you hadn't spoken out against Lord Sutherland in front of the Tory party members, he'd never have bowed to your later threat."

"Dora is right," Lord Audley added. "Most of what you and she do feels like fun and games. But every now and again, you will have to push yourself past the breaking point. The only thing that will sustain you in such moments is having a deeply held passion for our country. We don't need more yes men, no matter what the leading politicians might say. We need men and women who will stand in the way of those who would tear us apart."

Rex blushed again, his cheeks flaming to match the flickering fire behind him. But Dora felt certain he was chuffed to be the recipient of such glowing words from Lord Audley, a man not known for his effusive praise.

Mews, Rex's cheeky cat, chose that moment to make his presence known. He swiped a paw from underneath the sofa, batting the fringe hanging from Dora's skirt, and startled Dora's mother into a mild cry of alarm. She recovered soon enough and coaxed the cat out of its hiding place. She wasn't satisfied until Mews was curled in her lap, purring loud enough to be heard by all.

"You'll have to excuse Mama," Dora explained, chuckling under her breath. "You can take the girl off the farm, marry her to a duke, and have her dine with the king... but you can't take the farm out of the girl."

Lady Cavendish sniffed at her daughter's sassy remark. She leaned close to Mews, all the while scratching his chin, and said, "Don't mind her, precious baby. She's always been jealous of my ability to charm pets." She sat up and addressed the rest of the room. "I hope you'll forgive me for the faux pas of getting cat hair on my gown. We only intended to be in London for the weekend, and left our dogs at the manor. I have to admit, I miss them dreadfully. Now that all is resolved, we'll return to our idyllic life. Right, darling?"

Dora's father spluttered at his wife's question. "Well, you see, dear... With everything that's happened, I've had to rethink my position..." He stalled again and Lord Audley tapped him on his arm.

"Shall I take the fall for this one?" he offered.

Lord Cavendish flashed a grateful smile, but quickly covered it with a frown. "Yes, that's only right given you twisted my arm."

"Will one of you spit it out?" Dora intervened before the men could continue with their distraction.

Lord Audley shook his head at his protégé's lack of patience. "With Lord Sutherland locked away, and the case shushed up, the role of leader of the House of Lords became ever more important."

"Lord Godfrey was certainly keen," Rex said, cutting in.

Audley waved him off. "That was all for appearances. Godfrey prefers to call out japes from the back benches. He outright refused the opportunity. We needed a trustworthy man, impervious to offers of greater power and riches."

"Oh no," Lady Cavendish blurted, envisioning where this was going. "Absolutely not, Stephen. You promised me we'd spend our later years enjoying the peace of the countryside!"

"And we will," the duke cried. "But not just yet. Bonar Law is sure to be voted as Prime Minister. I promised to stick around long enough to help him get the government onto firm ground. When he departs, so will I. A year, tops."

"A year?" Lady Cavendish huffed out her frustration, dislodging the cat enough that he yowled in protest as well. "What about Benedict? He'll be none too happy to share the house with us again."

The image of her brother's reaction to the news was enough to bring a smile to Dora's face. No matter that the Cavendish London home had enough bedrooms to host a platoon. It wasn't the space invasion so much as it would place Benedict's single status back at the forefront of his mother's mind. With her under the same roof, he'd have to work triply hard to avoid being pushed to the altar.

That thought brought Dora endless amounts of amusement.

However, she sensed an intervention was needed, lest her father end up carved to ribbons in the dowager's drawing room. She wrapped an arm around her mother's shoulders. "Look on the bright side, Mama. If you're in London for an extended stay, this will give us more time to catch up, and for you to socialise with Lord Rex and my other friends."

"Err, about that..." Lord Audley's hesitant words caught everyone's attention. "While I wholeheartedly endorse everything Rex said at the Carlton Club, the fact remains that he called attention to himself. Given Rex doesn't have any intention of taking up a role in politics, at least not in the short term, he needs to disappear from society."

Rex nodded, his mouth turned down in a glum expression. "I'm being banished to Grandmama's Cotswold manor house. I'm terribly sorry, old girl, but you'll have to find someone else to escort you around for a while. I'm sure Clark is willing."

Dora tamped down her disappointment over Rex's impending absence. It made perfect sense for Audley to send him away for a while. She'd be fine on her own. She had Inga and Harris and the twins...

She repeated that thought in her head, but it didn't grow appealing no matter how she phrased it. She didn't want him to go. If he must, well... she wanted to go along with him.

The problem was convincing Lord Audley and her parents that this was a good idea. For someone as savvy as Dora, the task should have been a piece of cake.

But Dora's entire reason for being in London for such an extended visit was to reconnect with her parents. Lord Audley would certainly raise his eyebrows if she asked for a holiday from her sabbatical. Her mother would never let her live it down. Already, she'd caught her mother eyeing the two of them when she thought no one was watching.

Dora had no intention of hinting at her burgeoning romantic feelings for Rex. Especially not before she'd had the chance to discuss them with him.

She had one card up her sleeve. It was far from a trump card, as likely to cause her angst as provide a solution. But when stuck between Scylla and Charybdis, one had no choice but to choose the lesser of two evils.

Dora coughed lightly to get everyone's attention. She looked to Rex's grandmother. "Although it's impolite to discuss business at a dinner party, given we're all here and this is related to the current topic, I wondered if you might grant me some leeway, Edith?"

As expected, Rex's grandmother brushed Dora's question aside and encouraged her to speak.

"I received a telegram this afternoon from Count Vasile."

Lord Audley's eyebrows shot up. He was the only one who understood who Dora meant.

The dowager wasn't about to be left out. "I must say, I'm not familiar with the man. But if your tone is any clue, I should be."

Lord Audley came through with an explanation. "Count Vasile Zugravescu is his full name. He claims to be a distant relation of the Romanian royal family, but we've never found proof one way or the other."

"Why is this man sending you a telegram?" Dora's mother asked.

"We've rubbed shoulder at many a society event over the years. He said he was planning a visit to London and asked if I'd clear space in my diary to join him for supper. For old times' sake... whatever that means." Dora knew exactly what that meant, but it was not a fit topic for discussion with this group.

Lady Cavendish nodded at Dora and turned her gaze on Lord Audley. "Why would his visit be of interest to you?"

"Because we've long suspected the man of being a spy for hire. That last bit has made him almost impossible to pin down. With his ever-changing alliances, we had no idea which angles to monitor. Last time, we were sure he was ferrying messages from Greece to Russia, but shortly after the Spanish Communist party announced they received an influx of funding. We didn't even have Spain on our list."

Dora noted Lord Audley's exasperation. Her plan was certain to work. "What if we got solid, irrefutable proof of the man's secret activities? You could remove him from circulation, or add him as a tool in your arsenal."

Lord Audley puffed on his cigar and blew out a stream of smoke. "I'm listening..."

"I'll invite him out to the countryside for a house party. We can extend him the offer of adding people to the guest list. You know he prefers intimate environments where he can be in control, rather than running the risk of getting caught out by a large crowd."

"You want me to host," Rex said in a voice tinged with excitement. "Ducklington Manor would be ideal for such a pursuit. It's filled with secret hallways, hidey-holes, and—"

"Rex!" The dowager held up a hand to stave his flow of information. "There's no need for you to reveal my secrets to everyone! Suffice it to say, the house would be suitable for such an endeavour, should you choose to avail yourself of the property."

Dora had to cover her mouth with her hand to hide her laughter. She fought for control over her emotions and returned her gaze to Lord Audley when she could speak with a straight face. "What say you?"

Lord Audley glanced at Rex and Dora. The pair were certainly up to the task. He shrugged his shoulders and gave in to the inevitable. "What else can I say but yes?"

Dora's sense of satisfaction was so great that she launched straight into a discussion on the needed preparations.

Although she fancied herself the grand master of her own destiny, she made a fatal error.

The Dowager Duchess of Rockingham and the Duchess of Dorset locked eyes and exchanged secret smiles.

As the great Scottish poet Robert Burns proclaimed, "The best laid schemes o' Mice an' Men, Gang aft agley..."

While Dora and Rex monitored Count Vasile's every move, someone else would keep an eye on them.

* * *

BONUS EPILOGUE -

While Dora and Rex are occupied making plans for their visit to the Cotswolds, two others are busy plotting.

It all begins when the Dowager Duchess of Rockingham receives a handwritten invitation for an unusual meeting. To find out who she meets and what they discuss, grab your free copy of The Missing Agent bonus epilogue.

Claim your copy of the **BONUS EPILOGUE** here: https://view.flodesk.com/pages/645fcaa8a06058620b67631c

(*Note for existing newsletter subscribers - you can find the links to all my bonus scenes at the bottom of my weekly newsletter*)

Up next: Death Undercover

Want more Dora and Rex? Their story continues in Death Undercover. Read on for a sneak preview of the first chapter.

Don't need to read to know you want it? You can go ahead and order your copy of Death Undercover now on Amazon.

. . .

If you want to make sure you get notifications of all my releases, you can subscribe to my newsletter or follow me on Amazon:

Subscribe to my newsletter

Follow me on Amazon

Death Undercover
Here's your sneak preview of the first chapter

Theodora Laurent sat on the floor in the middle of her Belgravia bedroom, cushioned by the thick Persian carpet. The crackling flames in the nearby fireplace warmed the back of her silk pyjamas. Red velvet curtains, still closed against the weak morning sun, dampened the outside noise until all she heard was the ticking of the antique clock on the mantle and the periodic crack of the firewood. The only light in the room came from the pair of lamps on either side of the bed.

Dora sat with her legs crossed in a lotus shape and her hands resting on her knees. She'd learned this pose from an Indian yogi she'd met on her travels through the British empire. He'd promised her that taking a few minutes every day to quiet her mind would work wonders on her fortitude and grant her inner peace.

Dora made a point of undertaking a moment of silent meditation before setting off on any of her assignments. This one was particularly thorny, even if she had volunteered for it. In the coming days, her goal was to finally get proof that Count Vasile Zugravescu was a foreign spy.

The first time she'd met him, she'd been a newly minted

British spy with a code name and cover story... and her innocence. Her training had included everything except how to defend herself against her serious feelings of attraction. Count Vasile's smouldering dark looks and deluge of compliments had lit her heart on fire. In the wake of the Great War, far from almost everyone she knew, she was powerless against the desires he inflamed.

She'd dropped her guard and nearly lost her life in the process. If she hadn't stumbled across his plot to capture a British spy before he realised that spy was her, she'd be sitting now in some foreign prison.

Worst of all, it was pure, dumb luck she'd managed to get away. Not unscathed, however. She had a scar on her inner thigh and another on her heart to remind her of the price of blind love.

The next time their paths crossed, she'd looked at him with open eyes. In the fallow fields of her closed-off heart, she began having doubts about his dubious, if distant, claims to a foreign throne, and everything else he'd told her.

It was more likely that the name and title were a cover, just as Theodora Laurent was for her. But his employer and his actual history remained out of reach.

That infuriated her.

Again and again, they found themselves in the same place. Dora didn't dare let on to how much she knew. She danced cheek-to-cheek with him, barely keeping her balance as they walked along the knife's edge.

She transformed herself from an innocent young woman to a devious femme fatale. Yet she'd never caught him at a disadvantage. With no other choice, she'd done whatever was required to keep him from finding out her secrets.

Now the time had come for her to turn the tables. She'd uncover the answer to the question of his loyalties. Dora had arranged for the perfect set-up, offering to host him at a country house party. She'd have full control over the environment and every staff member on her payroll. Best of all, she'd have Rex, Inga, and the rest of her crack team with her.

It was a foolproof plan. She was positive it would go off without any issues.

And yet, she still suffered from a certain disquiet, all due to an unexpected gift.

Normally, the meditative practice delivered the results promised by the Indian yogi. With her palms facing upwards, ready to receive whatever the universe had in store for her, Dora had only to sit still, breathe deep, and listen.

Unfortunately, today, the universe had chosen to stick out its tongue at her request. She'd tried counting her breaths, pictured herself walking on a deserted path, and pretended to soar through the clouds. After a half hour of listening to the clock's infernal ticking, she'd resorted to conjugating irregular French verbs in her head.

Rather than getting closer, any hope of inner peace floated ever farther out of reach.

A knock on her bedroom door roused her from her reverie. "Stuff and nonsense," she muttered, groaning as her back twinged from sitting in one position for too long. She stood up. "Come in."

Her best friend and companion, Inga Kay, breezed through the doorway. She came to a sudden stop when her gaze landed on Dora. "You're still in your nightclothes? Rex is due to arrive in less than an hour and you haven't finished packing!"

"I'm nearly done," Dora countered, motioning toward the two giant travel chests sitting at the foot of the bed. "Cynthia did most of the work last night. I've only a few things to add. A quick change of clothes and I'll be ready."

"Hmm," was all Inga said in reply.

Dora hoped Inga would take the hint and leave her to get changed in peace, but the woman refused to budge. Instead, she wandered into Dora's dressing room to see for herself how much progress Dora had made.

"What is this?" Inga's voice echoed from the next room over. Dora froze in the alert pose of a deer hearing the first howls of the baying hounds. Mayhap if she didn't move, the danger would pass.

It was no use. Inga came to her.

Unlike Dora, Inga had dressed for a day of travelling in a simple wool dress in her favourite shade of dark red. She'd twisted her auburn hair into a tight coil to keep it from blowing in the wind during their drive. Inga held a hanger in her hand, with her arm lifted high enough to keep the pink fabric from dragging across the floor.

"Where in the world did this come from?" she asked.

Dora flicked her wrist at the empty box sitting on the desk.

Inga perked up at the sight of the white rectangular box. The telltale silver tissue paper peeking out from under the half-open lid proclaimed it to be from Dora's favourite couturière. Without a word, she laid the pink monstrosity of a gown across Dora's bed and dived into the box, looking for an explanation.

Inside, she found a thick, white card with a message penned in black ink. "From a fond admirer?" Inga spun around to gape at Dora. "That's it? Where's the rest of the message?"

"I think the dress is the rest of the message," Dora replied in a bone dry tone. She crossed the room to gaze upon the creation. "It arrived yesterday evening, while you and Harris were out."

The evening gown was cut in the latest fashion, sent over via special delivery from Paris. Made of pale pink satin, tiers of white chiffon decorated the skirt. The designer intended for it to hang loose enough to allow the owner to dance the night away.

Inga grimaced in distaste. "This isn't a dress. It's a wedding cake."

She wasn't wrong, even if Dora failed to be amused.

"Are you sure they didn't include it by mistake?"

Dora shook her head. "I sent Archie out with a telegram and told him not to leave the office until he got a reply. Monique confirmed. Someone ordered the dress via post and requested it be sent via courier. On the matter of who and why, she had no explanation."

"This may be the first time in my life I'm left speechless. This dress couldn't be less appropriate for you if it tried. If anything, the creation is better suited for an eighteen-year-old slip of a girl in her first season."

Dora didn't disagree with a word Inga said. She hadn't worn a dress that innocent since her earliest days as a spy, when she'd shed the last traces of her former life as Lady Dorothy.

Not since her initial encounter with Vasile.

It hadn't taken hours of contemplation for her to guess the identity of her so-called fond admirer. "I think Vasile sent this to me."

"Vasile?" Inga's head whipped around and she stared agog.

Dora gave a slow nod of confirmation. "He's reminding me of how we first met. How young I was. He's teasing me. The implied message is obvious. Theodora Laurent, society vixen, is now once again a tamed, clawless kitten."

Inga scrunched her brow and pondered Dora's words. "But he hasn't seen you in ages. How could he possibly think that? Not that I'm in any way suggesting it's true," she rushed to add.

Dora flicked the pink fabric, folding the gown over so she didn't have to look at its full glory. Even then, it continued to taunt her. She turned her back on it and flopped into the nearest chair to gaze up at the ceiling. "I'm in a quandary."

Inga strode over and stood directly behind Dora's chair,

leaning over so she forced Dora to look her in the eye. In a tone drier than the Sahara, she said, "You don't say."

Her deadpan delivery caused Dora to snort with laughter. She straightened up and waved to the nearby chair. "Sit down for a moment so we can discuss this like civilised people."

Inga took the proffered seat and helped herself to the now lukewarm tea. She lifted the ceramic teacup to her mouth, taking care to keep her pinky finger sticking out. "My lady, my time is yours." She punctuated her statement by taking a sip of the tea.

Her resulting expression of disgust had Dora laughing again. "I'm at a crossroads, Inga, and I don't know what to do with myself."

"I know we've tarried in England longer than you originally anticipated, but there's nothing holding us here. Is there?" Inga wagged her eyebrows.

"You're actually going to make me say the words?"

Inga nodded.

"Fine," Dora huffed. "I find Rex to be... intriguing."

"Is that how you young people call it today? It's only us hens here, so you might as well come right out and say it. You fancy Rex. I'm fairly certain he also fancies you. And that's fine. Go ahead, indulge. You'll be better once you get it out of your system. I'm hardly one to judge anyone's choice of partner. But that doesn't explain why you are letting Vasile's jest get to you."

"Because I've let my affection for Rex cause me to take my eye off the ball. We haven't stayed in one location this long since we left the war front. As for missions, even those are hardly our usual challenge." Dora sniffed. "I'm supposed to be England's greatest secret spy, and here I am cooling my heels in a Belgravia townhouse... by choice. By choice!" she huffed. "Maybe I should wear that pink dress."

"Over my dead body..." Inga mumbled into her teacup. She

glanced up to see Dora picking at her fingernail. It was time for an intervention. "Oh, do stop with the histrionics, Dora. So what that you've left the field, albeit temporarily? If Vasile thinks that means you're domesticated, then he's more addled than you are."

Dora removed the offending ragged fingernail from her mouth. She tilted her head enough to meet Inga's gaze. "Go on..."

Inga set her cup on the saucer and did as ordered. "Only someone who is a true master, who understands every aspect of their craft, can teach their skills to someone else. You've hardly sat around eating bonbons. Every single day you've got up and matched wits with Rex. Yes, he posed little challenge to start, but you can't deny his progress. You've studied, practiced, modelled, and tested yourself again and again. Personally, I can't wait until you have the last laugh."

Dora opened her mouth to rebut, but found herself with nothing to say. Of course, the woman was right! Dora gave herself a mental slap upside the head for not seeing the truth on her own.

But Inga wasn't done.

"All that said, there is another critical point I want you to take to heart."

Inga's tone was so serious that Dora shifted position until she was sitting up straight. "I'm listening."

Inga leaned forward and gathered Dora's hands in her own. "There is a universe of difference between soft and weak. Does the soft fur pelt of a lioness lessen the power of her bite? Does my love for Harris diminish my value to you? Throughout history, men have mistaken a woman's gentle affection for weakness. Yet, there is no greater fury than a woman aggrieved. Don't believe me? Try taking a babe from a mother's arms. Even the Bible says hell's power pales in comparison."

Lynn Morrison

The mantle clock chimed the half hour. Inga let their hands drop and stood to dispel the serious mood. "Time waits for no woman, and neither will our ride. Bring the dress and hang it where you will see it every time you enter your room. Let it serve as a reminder."

"Of my strength?"

Inga had her hand on the bedroom door. She glanced at Dora over her shoulder. "No, my friend. It is testament to Vasile's blind confidence. He has misled himself about the question of why you've stayed with Rex for this long. You'll prove him wrong. Mark my words — this trip will spell the end of his career."

Having said her piece, Inga left the room to track down the housemaid.

Dora sauntered into her dressing room. She scanned the contents of her wardrobe until she spotted the item she wanted.

Made of jet black lace, the front of the floor-length gown was decorated with gleaming beads and swirls of sequins. The neckline dipped low enough to raise eyebrows, while the cinched waist highlighted the wearer's slender physique. Only a thin lining protected the wearer's modesty. It was a gown for a queen of the night — a woman daring enough to walk the tightrope between flawless and fatally beautiful.

Dora pulled the dress from the rack and set it aside for Cynthia to pack. This was a gown meant for Theodora Laurent.

She'd wear the gown with pride. She'd show Vasile she was no tamed beast and instead was every bit as strong and determined as he remembered.

And if Rex tossed an extra glance her way, all the better. She'd finally best Vasile and then clear her schedule for a nice, long week or two with Rex. Far away from danger, she'd scratch that particular itch and then return to the field. Rex would be fully trained and ready to go his own way.

Her dilemma resolved, Dora raised her hands up to her chest and pressed her palms together. She closed her eyes, took a deep breath, and then released it with a long, cleansing sigh.

It turned out that the universe had an answer for her, after all.

Death Undercover

A Dora and Rex 1920s Mystery

They were sent to identify a spy in their midst. Instead, they'll have to unmask a murderer.

London, 1922. After their adventures at Westminster, Dora and Rex depart for a quiet break in the Cotswolds. Or at least, that's what everyone thinks.

In truth, they're working on a new assignment — investigating rumours that a titled foreigner might be more than he appears. Rex is to invite the man to his family manor for a rollicking weekend of fun. In between bouts of lawn tennis and parlour games,

he and Dora are to uncover the truth about the man's identity.

The servants barely have time to unpack everyone's case before the suspected spy is found with an antique dagger sticking from his back. With few suspects, the case shouldn't be too hard to solve. But when every door leads to a dead end, Dora and Rex are forced to consider a most unpalatable option.

Were they wrong in thinking the man was a foreign spy? Or... could someone else have a powerful motive for murder?

Order your copy of Death Undercover now on Amazon.

Historical Notes

On the 15th of September 1922, on the heels of Turkish victories in Izmir, the Daily Mail published an interview with Mustafa Kemal (later titled Atatürk). The interview made clear his demands - the Turks intended to take control of their capital city of Constantinople - either through force or negotiation. The final choice was left to the Allies. This set off a series of events known as the Chanak Crisis.

When I read about the twists and turns of this time in history, I knew I had to use it as the backdrop of my next mystery. It was certainly a case of fact being stranger than fiction.

In 1922, a coalition government ran the country, overseen by Prime Minister David Lloyd George. Formed on the heels of the end of World War I, the political parties agreed to put their differences aside in the best interest of recovering from the war. By 1922, patience and goodwill was in short supply. The Conservatives (Tories) were the largest party in Parliament. Lloyd George, however, was a Liberal. As tensions amongst the cabinet members grew, the Tories grew bolder in their attacks of Lloyd George's fitness for the role of Prime Minister.

Historical Notes

Although I'm no historian, based on everything I read, I firmly believe the government collapse was inevitable. That said, Lloyd Georges' choices on how to handle the Turkish threat certainly hastened his exit.

I stuck as true to the historical record as I could when crafting this tale, although I kept my focus on fictitious members of the House of Lords rather than using real people.

The Russian Rumour

Believe it or not, this part of the story was (mostly true) - false intelligence regarding potential Soviet support for the Turks did indeed fuel Lloyd George's fire for war. Although quickly proven to be false, Lloyd George and his trusted colleague Winston Churchill refused to let it go. Their outspoken support of patently false information proved to be an embarrassment to the government. (But, apparently not embarrassment enough to prevent Churchill's later rise to power.)

The Canadian Silence

When Lloyd George professed his determination to support the Greeks in a war against the Turks, there was no shortage of allies who disagreed. The one I found most interesting was Canada. Until this point in history, as a dominion of the UK, the Canadian Parliament followed wherever the UK government led. But with much of the world siding with the Turks, the Canadian Prime Minister Mackenzie King chose this moment to drag his heels on promises of aid.

Much like the UK leadership, the Canadian political parties split on the matter of the Greeks versus the Turks. By the time the matter could be debated in Parliament, the threat of war had passed.

Prime Minister King's actions fundamentally changed the relationship between the UK and Canada. No longer could the Dominion countries be relied upon for a blank cheque of support. The resulting discussions led to the 1931 Statute of Westminster which gave the Dominions the power to declare war on their own terms.

My Lord Audley is a fictional character and had nothing to do with the real events of the time. However, it took little imagination for me to see his invisible hand at work!

The Liberal Turncoat

Did you know that Winston Churchill, famous Conservative Prime Minister, was once a member of the Liberal party? I was fascinated to discover that he began his career as a Tory, crossed the aisle to join the Liberal party in 1904, and didn't return to the Conservative fold until 1924. I took that fact as a starting point for crafting my Liberal turncoat. The character of St Cecil and all of his actions within the book are entirely the product of my imagination.

The 1922 Committee

If you've followed the British political news between 2020-2022, you will likely have heard the term "The 1922 Committee" bandied about. While I do enjoy keeping abreast of the political intrigue of the day, I must admit I gave little thought to how this infamous Tory committee got its start.

After Lloyd George resigned and called for elections in late 1922, the Conservative party won by a landslide, bringing in a host of new blood. In April 1923, these newly elected MPs created a committee to meet weekly to encourage cooperation within the party.

In today's age, where the Tory party once again has a hold on the highest offices, the role of Prime Minister is still on uneasy footing. Since I moved to the UK in 2013, I've seen no less than four Conservative Prime Ministers move out of 10 Downing Street, all brought down by their own party members.

The Chairman of the 1922 Committee has responsibility for collecting and counting letters of no confidence from party

MPs. Anytime the count rises above 15% of party MPs (currently 54 letters), the Prime Minister faces a confidence vote on the House floor. In most cases, the threat of such an event is enough to provoke said Prime Minister into resigning. But in the days and weeks leading up to the final decision, the UK press loves to publish their guesses on exactly how many letters the Chairman holds in his desk drawer. In the age of the 24-hour news cycle, such guesses make for plenty of interesting discussions.

If you'd like to know more about the Chanak Incident, you can read THE CHANAK CRISIS AND THE BRITISH CABINET by J. G. Darwin in History, Vol. 65, No. 213 (1980), pp. 32-48 (17 pages).

If you'd like to know more about the 1922 Committee, The Hansard Society published a fascinating blog post written by Professor Stuart Ball, Emeritus Professor of Modern British History, University of Leicester, in honour of the committee's 100th anniversary: https://www.hansardsociety.org.uk/blog/the-1922-committee-what-are-its-origins

Acknowledgments

I'll begin as I always do, with a huge thanks to Ken Morrison and Anne Radcliffe for keeping me on the straight and narrow. Those two bear the burden of taking my early drafts and helping me shape them into the final product.

I also owe a word of thanks to Reagan Davis, Eryn Scott, Catherine Coles, Stella Bixby, and Julia Koty. There is something absolutely incredible about finding a community of people who are as excited and invested in your success as you are. Big thanks to Reagan and Eryn for giving me the space to talk out my plot knot from this book.

Donna L Rogers of DLR Cover Designs gets full credit for my fantastic series covers. If you saw my creative brief, you'd realise just how much trust I put into her work. She has yet to fail me!

Thanks to my husband and children for not getting too angry when I'm lost in my own world.

Thanks to my writing sprint group for keeping me company while I write. #TeamClark

Thanks to Brenda Chapman, Ewa Bartnik, and Fiona Birchall for beta reading the book and providing feedback to make it even better.

Last, a gigantic thank you to all my readers. I cannot tell you how much it means that you choose to spend some of your time and money reading my books.

About the Author

Lynn Morrison lives in Oxford, England along with her husband, two daughters and two cats. Born and raised in Mississippi, her wanderlust attitude has led her to live in California, Italy, France, the UK, and the Netherlands. Despite having rubbed shoulders with presidential candidates and members of parliament, night-clubbed in Geneva and Prague, explored Japanese temples and scrambled through Roman ruins, Lynn's real life adventures can't compete with the stories in her mind.

She is as passionate about reading as she is writing, and can almost always be found with a book in hand. You can find out more about her on her website LynnMorrisonWriter.com.

You can chat with her directly in her Facebook group - Lynn Morrison's Not a Book Club - where she talks about books, life and anything else that crosses her mind.

Also by Lynn Morrison

Raven's Storm

<u>Wandering Witch Urban Fantasy</u>

A Queen Only Lives Twice

Made in the USA
Monee, IL
07 July 2023

38774937R00132